#LetsALLBeKind
xo
Marie Unanue

THE ADVENTURES OF PHATTY AND PAYASO
CENTRAL PARK

THE ADVENTURES OF PHATTY AND PAYASO
CENTRAL PARK

MARIE UNANUE

iUniverse®

THE ADVENTURES OF PHATTY AND PAYASO
CENTRAL PARK

iUniverse books may be ordered through booksellers or by contacting:

iUniverse
1663 Liberty Drive
Bloomington, IN 47403
www.iuniverse.com
1-800-Authors (1-800-288-4677)

ISBN: 978-1-5320-4051-1 (sc)
ISBN: 978-1-5320-4053-5 (hc)
ISBN: 978-1-5320-4052-8 (e)

Library of Congress Control Number: 2018903573

Printed in the United States of America.

iUniverse rev. date: 04/30/2018

CONTENTS

Let's All Be Kind.

To my husband, Andy.
Because of you, I believed in myself.
Because of you, I reached for the stars. And
because of you, I am able to grab them.
Because of you, I know love.
Because of you, I am forever thankful and eternally grateful.

To Jackie Bezos.
You believed in me from day one, and you never stopped.
You gave me courage when I had none.
You gave me confidence when I had little.
And above all, you gave me friendship and love.
To the moon and back, my dear friend.

To Mom and Dad.
It only takes meeting either of you for one second to
understand why I'd write a book about kindness. You
are the very definition of the word. Thank you for
not only believing in me but also teaching me right
from wrong and the importance of kindness.
I love you both.

CHAPTER 1

Phatty was perched with his big belly balanced atop his favorite army-green armchair. His fat—or, as he called it, his "splendid undercarriage"—hung over the sides of the chair like excess dough that had been squished out of a baker's pan. He let out a deep, relaxing yawn, followed by his typical gymnast stretch, his front and back paws extending. Then, as quickly as the stretch began, Phatty released it, and his legs once again dangled down. Although it was certainly not the most flattering position for a cat of his size and stature, Phatty felt like a king.

His chair had seen better days. The green velvety material that covered the plush seat and back had been worn thin from years of Phatty's daily routine. The chair arms were tattered, and where there was material left, it was dull and pulled from Phatty's back claws. Phatty's parents kept the chair, despite its ragged look, because they knew how much Phatty loved it.

Phatty squinted up into the sunlight that warmed his entire body as a cool breeze blew through his whiskers. Breathing deeply, Phatty could smell the spring flowers. The strong odor of gardenias told him that spring was in full bloom in Central

Park. Today, the sun would warm the ground in the park, and he knew the plants would come alive.

Phatty loved to hear all about Central Park, and although he had never experienced it firsthand, he lived for every detail that others shared with him and whatever he could see while he spent hours gazing out his large living room windows. Phatty's brother Stanley was taken to the park daily for walks and always came back with a new story and experience to share. Phatty could see so much of the park from his nineteenth-floor terrace and his chair. He loved the rosebush trellis that his mother doted on, its vivid red and pink flowers trailing up and over the arbor in stunning display. But it did block his view sometimes, so the details about the many ponds and waterfalls, the fields, the old buildings, and, of course, the Central Park Zoo and merry-go-round came from those who had been in the park themselves. He imagined the poets on Poets Walk, forever frozen in stone for people to enjoy.

But however beautiful Central Park was during the day, this mysterious forest became an entirely different experience at night. After sunset, Central Park looked so gloomy and dark that even high up on his terrace Phatty was terrified by the sight of it. He shivered as he pictured animals stalking in the shadows and late-night park dwellers wandering through the blackness while raccoons and rats reigned.

Normally, on a beautiful morning like this, Phatty would love nothing more than to watch the action in Central Park, but today he was having trouble just sitting still. On this day, after months of waiting, his best friend, Payaso—the cat who lived across the hall for a few months each year—was finally coming back to town.

Nothing could ruin my day, thought Phatty. He took a deep breath and purred loudly. *Today is going to be "fan-tabby-lous."* Phatty smiled, impressed with himself and his own made-up word.

Fan-tabby-lous, Phatty thought, giggling again. *Wait until I tell Payaso this one!* Phatty closed his eyes, still giggling at his own joke.

Pleased with himself, Phatty drew in a deep breath just as a strong breeze blew in the terrace window.

Snap! A photo slammed down on the piano. Phatty shot up at the sharp sound, his heart racing, and frantically searched for a place to hide. Just as he was about to dive off his throne, he noticed the photo frame lying on its side.

It was just the wind, you scaredy-cat! Taking a deep breath, Phatty tried to rebalance himself on his perch, but to his horror, he felt himself starting to teeter.

Phatty gulped as he pursed his lips and puckered his whiskers. Desperate to regain his balance, he frantically clawed at the chair's fabric as he began sliding down its side. It was useless: gravity controlled the downward momentum of his thirty-pound frame. His big belly rolled and squished as he toppled over. Landing like a rock, he heard the air expel from his lungs with a loud *whoosh*. Momentarily dazed, he shook his head hard, trying to clear his jumbled vision. Bouncing up, he meowed as he quickly looked around to see if anyone had witnessed his fall from grace.

Phew. Nobody. Then, as if nothing had happened, Phatty licked his paws, flattened his whiskers, and sat up straight, smoothing down his tousled belly fur. He frowned as he took a deep breath to compose himself and reflect on his fear. He had always been an awkward cat (there was no denying that), and he had come to terms with his unbalanced and pudgy demeanor. But in moments like this, he felt even worse about himself—scared of everything, overweight, and about as graceful as a blindfolded hippo on ice skates.

Putting his head down on his front paws, he sighed. *Well, even Beyoncé fell off a stage once or twice!* Closing his eyes, he pictured Beyoncé. *She's bootylicious too!* He giggled now as he pictured himself falling down the back of the chair, in his own "bootylicious" way, bumping and crashing all the way down.

Still giggling, eyes still closed, Phatty took in the warm sun as he made a mental note to add this incident to the long list of things to tell Payaso.

Crack! Crack! Rap! A sharp tapping on the window jolted Phatty's eyes open and immediately sent him back into self-defense mode.

Before Phatty could react, he noticed a large black shadow creeping across the floor—a paralyzing sight that left him stricken with fear.

The shadow froze. "What's wrong, kitty? You're not giggling anymore. What is it? *Cat* got your tongue?"

Phatty looked up. A dark, menacing hawk stood on the terrace and shrieked with enjoyment at his own joke. Phatty squealed, his own ears shocked at the sound that escaped him.

The hawk continued. "Poor kitty. What is it? All of a sudden your joke is no longer funny?"

Too scared to look at the creature any longer, Phatty looked away—and noticed a second shadow that was bigger and rounder, like a porcupine. It mimicked his every move! *Wait,* Phatty realized. *That's my shadow.* He felt relieved, but not for long.

"Hey, kitty! I'm over here!" the hawk called out. "Hello? It is rude not to look at someone when he is speaking to you. Don't you have any manners? Come on—why don't you share the joke with me?" asked the hawk sarcastically.

Phatty didn't move or answer, just quivered in his chubby frame.

"Tsk. Tsk. Tsk. Okay, well, suit yourself then, but I do have to tell you I find it so sad, you sitting there all alone laughing at your own jokes. *So* pitiful."

Phatty was now standing, but his legs wobbled out from under him as he tried to take a step.

"Don't move on my account, fat cat!" said the hawk. "That is your name, correct? *Fatty* the cat? You can tell so much by a name—do you not agree? Oh yes, I know all about names from those loser animals over at the zoo."

"It's *Phatty* spelled with a *P-H,* not an *F,*" Phatty hollered. His own voice was so loud it surprised not only him but also the hawk. The giant bird squawked and ruffled his feathers haughtily.

Phatty took one awkward step, as if testing out his legs, and then stopped.

The hawk cackled and said, "Going to hide, are you? Don't hide on my account. I mean, come on. I can get you no matter where you hide, and I do prefer seeing you spread out on the floor like a doormat."

Phatty was used to teasing. Small birds in the neighborhood often teamed up and picked on him when he was lounging on the terrace, chasing him inside. But today was different. Today, he was face-to-face with a big, ferocious hawk—one powerful enough to pick up Phatty and whisk him away. The hawk's talons, sparkling in the sunlight, looked as sharp as razors.

The hawk shrieked again, making Phatty jump. Without meaning to, he looked right into the hawk's steely blue-gray eyes. Phatty had no doubt that he was staring down the meanest and largest hawk in the entire park.

"What's your name, flyboy?" asked Phatty, trying to muster some bravado. Venturing closer, Phatty took in every inch of the menacing bird. The creature's beak and left talon were a mangled mess—the most hideous-looking features Phatty had ever seen. What could have caused a beak to twist that way or a talon to look like a crushed grape?

"I'm Crawler," the hawk bellowed.

For a second, Phatty's fear melted into pity as he imagined the horrible and painful event that had caused Crawler's deformities. *Was it a trap? Or maybe a flying accident?* Phatty's curiosity consumed him as he peered directly into the hawk's eyes.

For three seconds, they sat motionless, staring at each

other. Phatty tried to imagine the bird's past. He tilted his head with compassion and opened his mouth to ask the bird what had happened—

"Sqqqquuaaak!" Crawler screamed.

Phatty leaped what felt like ten feet into the air. The sound was so shrill and so horrendous that Phatty's paws scrambled faster than his mind, and he instinctively clawed himself across the floor to his hiding spot.

Crawler sounded enraged now as he blared, "Get a good look at me, dough boy, because in the next couple of days, you're going to be seeing a whole lot of me! By Wednesday night, I am coming in for you and your family and your furry little friends." Crawler finished off the threat with an evil cackle.

Terror washed over Phatty, leaving him trembling and weak.

"Not so brave and big now, are you, kitty?" the hawk continued. "Where is your brother or your puppy dog now to protect you? You don't think this little screen can stop me from getting in, do you? They couldn't keep me locked in at the Central Park Zoo, so what makes you think this thin screen can stop me now?"

Bang. Bang. Bang. Crawler slammed his beak and talons against the window screen; it sounded louder than even the pounding of Phatty's heart. As the hawk continued to beat away at the screen with his huge talons, one section at a time, Phatty's blood ran cold.

Halfway to his hiding spot, Phatty kicked it into high gear, unable to risk another second out in the open. His paws began to slide out from under him as he crossed the hardwood floor. With one long, loud, deep breath—and with all the courage he had left—Phatty dove full speed under the couch, where he could hide safely.

"Do you know what I am going to do to you when I get inside your house, Phatty? I think you do, don't you, fatty cat?"

The hawk squawked as he pecked faster and faster. "You won't be able to hide from me under the couch, because I will be coming for you. I am going to pick you apart, and when I am done, I will find your brothers and feed them piece by piece to the other birds—and after that, I will get what I came for: your mother's jewels!"

Then, in that next instant, the pecking abruptly stopped. A moment of eerie silence followed. Phatty squeezed himself into a tight ball under the couch and held his breath, desperate to hear anything that indicated the hawk's next move. Despite the discomfort of the couch springs digging into his back, he remained frozen in place, listening. Straining as hard as he could, he still heard nothing—not other birds chirping, not horns honking down on the street, not even the sound of the wind rustling through the trees in the park. It was as if time had stopped and at that moment, the world stood just as frozen as Phatty.

As the silence dragged on, Phatty started shaking uncontrollably. He was forced to let out his breath and began gasping for air. Other than his own panting and the pounding of his heart in his ears, Phatty heard nothing. Maybe the hawk had already broken the screen! Maybe he was already inside! Tears welled up in Phatty's eyes. Then, in a frantic attempt to hear anything, he took another deep breath and held it, just as the flap on the couch was lifted.

"What are you doing now, Phat Boy?" his brother Clyde asked as he stuck his head under the couch, exposing Phatty to the sunlight.

"Aaauuuggggghhhh!" Phatty screamed.

Clyde was so startled by the scream he jumped back a foot, knocking a figurine off the table and sending it crashing loudly to the floor. *"Eeeaaaak!"* Clyde's front paws clapped down over his own mouth out of embarrassment at the shriek that had just escaped his lips.

"For the love of catnip!" Clyde finally growled from behind

his paws. Normally a brave cat, he picked himself up and shook his startled head. "What in heaven's name is going on, Phatty? You almost gave me a heart attack!" Clyde glared at his clearly frightened brother.

Phatty's sweet little eyes were squeezed shut, and he was shaking harder than Clyde had ever seen. Clyde's heart broke at the very sight of him. He reached in to caress Phatty with one paw and said as softly as he could, "Phatty, I'm here. Calm down. What has you this upset?"

Obviously too scared to open his eyes or speak, Phatty mouthed the words silently: *Look behind you. The big hawk Crawler is at the window!*

Clyde turned around and saw nothing but an open window and a torn screen. Clyde grew angry when he realized that Crawler the hawk was to blame. He'd heard about the bird bully from his friends who'd been to the park.

"Phatty, he's gone now. Please come out."

"No, I'm fine under here, thanks," Phatty mumbled.

"I promise, he's gone, and I won't let him hurt you," Clyde said softly again, trying to keep his temper under control.

"He said he was going to hurt us! Feed you to the birds! And …" Phatty was crying too hard now to go on.

"Come on, Phatty! Come out. Don't let that silly hawk ruin your day. After all, you have been talking my ear off about today for what feels like years." Clyde knew that Payaso was the one thing that could make his brother feel better.

"He said he was coming for us and for mom's jewels!" Phatty gasped. "I thought he was inside. I could hear him tearing the screen, and when it stopped, I thought he had gotten into our home!"

Clyde reached in and placed his paw on Phatty. "Please, come on out. I'm looking at the window, and he is definitely gone." Clyde let go of Phatty's paw and sought to reassure him by climbing up onto the window ledge. Clyde flexed his long, lean body and closed the window.

While thinking about the hawk, Clyde pinched his lips tightly together, silently fuming. There had been many rumors about this crazed hawk, and now Clyde knew for certain they were true. Word was this flying creature—oddly enough named Crawler—had escaped from his new home in the Central Park Zoo. The zoo had acquired the bird after it was injured. Bird gossip was that the hawk could do multiple tricks and was as well trained as any animal in the circus. Now living on the lam, he was mixed up with a very bad man—one who used the hawk's talents to break into people's homes.

"It's actually quite brilliant," Clyde admitted to Phatty. He imagined the hawk and the man working together. "He can simply enter through open windows and steal whatever valuables he can find: cash, jewelry, anything he can carry in that big ol' beak or his talons. It's the perfect crime, because unless somebody walks in and sees him flying away covered in jewels, nobody can prove the bird's or the man's guilt."

"And now, he plans to steal mom's jewels!" Phatty sighed, still wedged in his hiding place.

This only confirmed the bird was a thief. But worse than that, Clyde thought, Crawler was also a bully who only tormented the weak. That, Clyde was most certain, was about to end.

Clyde scanned for the hawk as he stretched himself in the center of the large picture window that overlooked not only the front terrace but also the entire park, careful to flex his back muscles in a way that showed them off. Although Phatty and Clyde were brothers, Clyde wasn't built anything like Phatty. Clyde was very tall, with robust broad shoulders, long legs, and an air of confidence. At a solid twenty-four pounds, he was a mixture of lean muscle and sturdy, solid bones, with a glossy fur coat that shined in the sunlight. He knew he was not just any cat; he was the kind of cat that no bird of any size should ever dare to mess with.

If there was one thing Clyde wouldn't take, it was anyone

bullying his brothers. Clyde surveyed the terrace and saw no sign of the mischievous flying pest. Then he carefully glanced from tree to tree down in the park. He could still hear Phatty's loud panting from deep under the sofa as he scanned for any sight of this heinous bird. Clyde knew, right then and there, it would be his mission to ensure that this hawk would not terrorize his brother another second.

CHAPTER 2

It was some time later when Phatty finally felt brave enough to peek out from under the couch. He could see Clyde jumping gracefully from window ledge to window ledge. Phatty was in awe of Clyde's balance and, more than that, Clyde's constant state of balance as he leaped. Clyde never looked frightened; he seemed always sure he wouldn't fall, and despite the height or distance of the jump, Clyde's expression was one of pure confidence.

When Phatty jumped or leaped, he closed his eyes, bunched up his whiskers, and heaved himself into the air. As if thirty pounds of fat cat wasn't hard enough to look at, the fear plastered on Phatty's face was sufficient to make anyone scramble out of the way. But Clyde showed no such fear. He was like a tiger at the zoo as he patrolled his own perimeter, ready to take on anyone or anything that dared get in his way.

"He's gone, Phatty," Clyde reaffirmed.

"You believe me about Crawler, right?" Phatty asked, looking up at Clyde.

"Of course I do," Clyde said. "And you should know more than anyone that eventually I am going to eat that flying bully for breakfast. Remember, Phatty, each time he scares you or picks on you, it's to make him feel better about himself. Just wait until I get ahold of him! If he ever finds his way into this house—well, let's just say that would be the end of him bullying you." Clyde's voice was harsh, and he ended with a growl.

Phatty knew he meant those words.

"Crawler said he'll have all of mom's jewels by Wednesday!" Phatty paused and then continued. "I saw his face too—he's a mangled mess. His eyes … they looked at me in such a way …" Phatty shivered now as he spoke. "I can tell he'll stop at nothing to get in here! He said the zoo couldn't keep him locked up. The stories must be true, Clyde! He came from the zoo."

"Calm down, Phatty," Clyde said with more patience than usual. "I don't know what to believe about this Crawler, but letting him scare you is not the answer. If he came from the zoo, the zoo must be looking for him. They'll find him."

"I just wish there was a way to get him back to the zoo or a way to tell the zoo where he is." Phatty sighed and plopped down on the floor. He hunched over, feeling very defeated.

"Hey," Clyde said, breaking the silence in the room. "What time will that fur ball next door get here?"

Phatty's head popped up at the question—it had done the trick of distracting him from his fears and worries.

"Soon!" Phatty purred. He smiled at the sight of his brother, sitting at the window, watching for Crawler. All Phatty's life, Clyde had protected him, shooing away anyone and anything who scared Phatty. Phatty rested his head on his paws, let a deep sigh escape, and closed his eyes, drifting off to sleep, once again happy. He didn't need much to make him happy, and he didn't care about fancy things. In his world, all he needed was what he liked to call the three fabulous Fs: food, family, and friends.

A few hours later, Phatty was startled awake by the sound of the wind knocking over a flowerpot on the terrace. When his eyes opened, he could see Clyde asleep now in the big window. Phatty stretched his legs out and then carefully climbed down from the top of his chair. He took a deep breath. He could still smell the remnants of his mom's famous turkey meat loaf from the night before. Phatty loved when she cooked. The house would smell like magic for days.

Phatty strained to listen, but with the windows closed, the only sound he could hear was that of the Manhattan traffic nineteen floors below. He heard the occasional horn blow and the boom from a large truck as it hit one of Manhattan's many potholes. It was a familiar symphony—one he loved. It was the sound of New York, the city that never slept, the city he adored.

He wanted to check the time, so he made his way to the kitchen clock. He knew, thanks to his canine brother, Stanley, to wait for the chimes to ring, and that meant it was a new hour. Stanley taught him to imagine the clock was a big pizza pie. When there was a straight line down the middle of the pie, cutting it in half, it meant his parents were going to be home. When the pie had only one little slice in it, from the top down, it meant that it was lunchtime. Today, Stanley had told him that if the pie looked like an *L*, it meant Payaso was due to arrive.

It wasn't quite an *L* yet, but it was close, so Phatty watched the front door, practically willing the familiar knock to come. He remembered the first time Payaso had knocked on his door many years ago and smiled.

Payaso had only been a kitten when he first came to Phatty's door in search of new friends. His family was in town for a few months, and he was lonely and hoping to find someone to play with—especially after he learned that two cats and a little dog lived across the hall. Every day, Payaso knocked on Phatty's door, said hello, and looked under the door to see what was going on. The space was just big enough for two eyes and a crooked neck to see in.

"What's your name?" Payaso had asked after the fourth visit. When no answer came, Payaso decided he would introduce himself. Phatty could still remember Payaso telling him about his name. "*Payaso* means 'clown' in Spanish," Payaso giggled. "Though I do not fancy myself anything of the sort!"

From that day on, Payaso would peer under the door, say hello, and wait for anyone to give him attention. Each time, he would share details about the different activities he had done that day—from books he had read to movies he had seen and just about any other topic on which he could muse. Not only could he see Phatty sitting in his apartment, inching closer every visit to the front door, but Payaso could also hear Phatty's gasps or chuckles during his stories, telling him that Phatty was listening to every word.

Truth be told, even though he didn't say it, Phatty couldn't wait for Payaso to arrive each day. He had started to look forward to the newest travel tale or book review. Phatty had never known such an intelligent and exotic cat. To Phatty, who was just a tabby, Payaso seemed glamorous and distinguished. If there were an animal directory, Payaso's photo would be right there under "Renowned" as far as Phatty was concerned.

Phatty wasn't sure what was most fascinating about Payaso: Was it his stubby "bobbed" tail or his long mane of fur, regal and lionesque? Or was it his hind legs that appeared longer than his forelegs, making him walk with an odd but empowering swagger?

If Phatty had to pick, it would be Payaso's large, round feet, which looked almost bearish. That and how Payaso could use his thumbs to flush the toilets! Phatty laughed, imagining the scene. Payaso once explained that his feet were equipped with the famous bobtail signature "toe tufts"—an extra tag of skin on the paws that stuck out to the side, resembling a thumb. As if having thumbs on his feet were not cool enough, Payaso could read, write, and speak several languages, and he had traveled the world with his parents.

After a few weeks of Payaso's introductory monologues, he squeezed his favorite catnip toy under the front door for Phatty to play with. As soon as Phatty thought no one was around, he grabbed the toy and played with it for hours.

Payaso's gesture of goodwill had built up enough courage in Phatty to wait at the door. The next day, when Payaso knocked, Phatty quietly whispered "hello" before running back under the couch.

"Maybe tomorrow we can play?" Payaso asked excitedly from the doorway. But he heard no response and turned to go home.

"Okay," came Phatty's muffled voice from under the couch. "See you tomorrow."

Payaso was so happy Phatty had finally agreed to play with him that he jumped joyfully back to his apartment. Payaso understood Phatty must be very shy, which probably meant he had difficulty making friends. Payaso decided he would do whatever he could to help Phatty come out of his shell.

The next day, Payaso came over and lightly knocked again. Without wanting to give Phatty a chance to hide or change his mind, he jumped up onto the doorknob and, using his toe tufts and all of his strength, turned the knob and opened the door. Payaso had never had any trouble opening doors, but this one was heavier than he had realized. It had taken all of Payaso's momentum to turn the knob, and when the door swung open with speed, Payaso went flying into Phatty's foyer. He landed with a loud thump and then slid across the floor into a table, causing it, and everything on it, to crash over.

"Hello, everyone!" Payaso said, as if he had landed exactly the way he had intended. He stood up, casually brushed himself off, kicked the remnants of a lamp out of his way, and strode right into the living room. Phatty had never seen anything like it. He was in awe. Clyde, on the other hand, wasn't as thrilled by the other cat's entrance. Clyde screamed for an hour about the broken lamp and the audacity of anyone who would just open up a door without permission.

Phatty and Payaso ignored Clyde's rant and played for the first time for hours. Before they knew it, they'd become the very best of friends. Whenever Payaso was in town, the pair were inseparable—so inseparable that on some days, their parents left the front doors open so the cats could play. They quickly learned everything about each other, and although they were opposite in every way, they got along effortlessly.

Now, all these years later, Phatty couldn't imagine his life without Payaso. They were not just best friends; Phatty considered Payaso family. And Phatty knew that Payaso would jump on board to help him protect his family.

Phatty would have to concentrate now about what to do next about Crawler so he'd have ideas to discuss with Payaso. Normally, he would have spent the next hour daydreaming about what he and Payaso would do this trip, but after his frightening morning, he knew that today he had bigger fish to fry. That fish's name was Crawler.

First, he would tell Payaso all about his run-in with the hawk. Then he would work up the nerve to tell his best friend all about the idea he had to set "Crawler traps" throughout the apartment to protect his brothers and his friend. With Payaso's assistance, they could booby-trap the house to alert Phatty whenever the hawk came to his window so Phatty could find someone to help. He couldn't wait to share his idea with Payaso, and when he pictured Crawler meeting Payaso for the first time, Phatty laughed as he thought to himself, *Oh, how that hawk has a thing or two coming!*

CHAPTER 3

When Clyde woke from his afternoon nap, he saw Phatty smiling, sitting alone, giggling, and staring aimlessly at a blank spot on the wall.

"Are you still waiting for that fur ball to get here?"

Phatty jumped, obviously startled.

"Ahemmm." Phatty cleared his throat, his fur scrunching up with embarrassment. "What is taking Payaso so long?"

Clyde walked over to his brother and asked, "Why don't you do something useful with yourself instead of obsessing over that cat?"

"I have been!" replied Phatty. Excitedly, he explained his plan to booby-trap the apartment.

"Booby traps?" Clyde asked, hardly able to hide his laugh at the sound of that ridiculous word. "*Booby traps*? Well, congratulations. That sounds about as ridiculous as when you and that know-it-all fur ball came up with the harebrained idea to talk in secret code to each other!" Clyde said, watching to see if he could read his brother's response. How Clyde wished his brother would listen to him for once, lose some weight, and gain some confidence rather than hide behind secret codes, traps, and other bizarre schemes he and his fur-brained friend concocted. "Phatty, you can't live in fear your whole life."

"Our secret codes fooled you, Clyde," Phatty said, beaming with pride. "Not even you or Stanley could figure out what we were talking about!" Phatty's voice began with certainty, but it wavered at the end of his retort.

"Oh, I'm sorry. I forgot you fooled a seven-pound dog." Clyde cleared his throat and spoke louder. "May I remind you again, *a dog*. Hardly something to go bragging about, Phatty. As for fooling me, I wasn't even listening to your chatter and games. You can't fool someone who is not playing along or doesn't even care."

Phatty and Payaso had come up with a way to talk secretly in public. One would start to refer to a past story or experience he had shared, using as little detail as possible, and immediately the two friends would be on the same page. Phatty smiled as he remembered Payaso asking if he could use the litter box in front of Clyde.

"Uh, Phatty," Payaso had whispered with urgency, "do you remember that thing that Clyde hates that I use when I come here? Well, I need to use it. Like now. It's a stage two kind of emergency, if you catch my drift …"

Phatty immediately went to distract Clyde so Payaso could use the box in peace and privacy. Neither Clyde nor Stan ever caught on … well, not until the smell filled the entire apartment. Still, Phatty still felt victorious about their secret language.

"Why don't you exercise, or organize your toys, or clean up your litter box?" Clyde urged. "Don't just waste your day waiting for that cat to get here."

Phatty shrugged. "I think Payaso's impending arrival just makes you grouchy. You don't have any friends, and as the years have passed, your loathing of Payaso has only become more obvious."

"Hummmpppfff," Clyde responded and then turned his back and began grooming vigorously.

"Clyde," Phatty kept on, "you don't get it. I can't do anything else! I've been counting down the days for months, and today is the day!" He tried to roll himself off his back and onto his feet in one swift motion, but midroll, Phatty lay like a distressed turtle on his back, with his large, rotund belly oozing onto the floor. Slowly he managed to lean to his right side and then stand.

"What is the big deal about that cat anyway?" Clyde snapped. "If you ask me, he is annoying with that know-it-all attitude. 'Au revoir! Adios! I learned this! Did you know that?' I'd like to find a way to shut his big mouth ..."

A commotion at the door interrupted Clyde's tirade. Phatty, hoping Payaso was finally there, ran to the front door as it opened, his heart thumping with excitement.

"Hello, Phatty!" His dog brother, Stanley, came barreling in, full of his usual energy and smelling of the streets. Stanley's dog-walker was bringing him home from his walk, and Stanley circled around the boy, barking for a treat. Stan was a fun-loving dog adored by both animals and people. Aside from being a dog, Phatty couldn't think of a single bad thing to say about him. While he loved Stan, however, he couldn't help but feel disappointed to see him standing there rather than Payaso.

"You should have seen what was going on outside today!" Stan enthused as the dog-walker unleashed him. "Man oh man, was it a great day to be in the park! There was that crazy squirrel again, and these big, chubby, pooping birds, and tons of other dogs! I was running and—"

"Save it, Stan," interrupted Phatty, who was eyeing the dog-walker with caution. "You tell me the same thing every day, but I'm not in the mood to hear it right now. I've got more important things to focus on. I'm waiting for Payaso to get here." With that, Phatty turned and walked away.

"Oh. Sorry," mumbled Stanley, looking down at his paws.

"He'll be here soon, Phatty. Don't you worry." Phatty knew that Stan had lots of friends he often saw at the park, so the dog didn't understood that Payaso was his brother's only friend.

Phatty was sorry that he'd interrupted Stanley, especially since the dog had meant no harm by sharing the details of his fun outing. The cat was about to apologize to Stanley when he realized the dog-walker had forgotten that when the door was open, it was supposed to stay open. The dog-walker must have closed the door out of habit.

Another dreadful event!

Phatty's heart sank. What else could go wrong today? Deciding he would apologize to Stanley later, Phatty rolled on his back and stared at the ceiling as he continued to wait for his friend. Nothing else mattered to him but how slowly the time was passing.

2x4
5 3
7
+

CHAPTER 4

Phatty had awakened from his sulk nap and was watching the clock when he finally heard the familiar sound. There was no doubt that it was Payaso's voice burbling across the hallway through Phatty's door. Phatty's heart pounded with disappointment as he remembered again that the front door was closed.

Just as he began to panic, he heard the best sound: the sound of the doorknob turning and Payaso's mom's sweet voice as she opened the door for the animals to play.

"Who's very handsome, loves treats, and has *thumbs*?" yelled Payaso as he skidded through the doorway. "Me! I'm back! What's happening?" Payaso laughed.

Phatty leaped off the couch and ran over to say hello to his friend. Finally, his day was turning around! Payaso was not in the house two seconds before he and Phatty were laughing and swapping stories about what had happened while they were apart. It was hard to imagine how they were able to still breathe, given how quickly they spoke to each other—paws flying, whiskers whistling, and mouths flapping and smiling.

Payaso couldn't wait to teach Phatty all the new words he'd learned since he'd been gone.

"We'll have all sorts of adventures now that I'm back," Payaso explained as he gave Phatty an affectionate head butt. "I've got plans, man, big plans!"

After they caught up, Payaso listened earnestly to Phatty as he filled Payaso in on the situations with the nasty birds and Crawler, especially about what had happened with the hawk earlier in the day.

"So, Payaso, I need your help. Will you read up about booby-trapping tonight and help me come up with some ideas? After today, with Crawler, I'm almost too scared to sleep or eat. Well …" He stopped. Looking down at his big body, he became embarrassed. "But today, I couldn't eat. Imagine that! Please! Please help me build booby traps."

Payaso leaned back, his expression a bit askance. "Well, all right then. Anything to make you feel better."

"Thanks, Payaso! You're a true friend."

"I can just picture you squeezed under the couch, hunched over and frightened to death. I know you're scared of the small birds; I can only imagine your fear of a big hawk. Tomorrow," Payaso said, "first thing in the morning, we'll begin planning how to stop this madness. You know, Phatty, I'd do anything to help you. Tonight I'll read up about booby traps, hawk habits, and bird diseases on my Kindle Fire so we will have plenty of ideas!"

"Bird diseases? Why?" Phatty asked with concern. "I don't want to poison or hurt the birds or the hawk. I just want them to leave me alone," Phatty said quietly.

"Of course we won't hurt them, Phatty," Payaso said reassuringly. "We won't hurt anything. I just want to make sure those flying, flapping, big-beaked, noisy nuisances can't give us any creepy, fur-eating, whisker-crunching diseases!"

"Man, you are so smart, Payaso," Phatty said as he beamed with pride.

For the rest of the day, it was business as usual for Phatty and Payaso. They chased toys, played, napped, and told stories. Before they knew it, Payaso's mom was calling across the hall for him to come home for dinner. He had been traveling cross-country from Seattle all day, and even though he hated to admit it, he was tired and ready for bed.

"How did the day go by so fast?" Phatty asked. "Before you got here, that clock seemed to be ticking an hour per second!" The disappointment was clear in his voice.

"Don't worry," Payaso reassured him. "I'll be back first thing tomorrow, and we'll start working on Operation Hawk-Be-Caught!"

Payaso's mom called for him again as she strode through the front door. When Clyde heard Payaso's mom at the door, he immediately perked up and raced to say hello to her. Clyde absolutely adored Payaso's mom.

"Move it, fur ball," Clyde mumbled as he pranced past Payaso at full speed. Phatty watched as Payaso's mom bent down to pet Clyde, giving him a few delicious treats.

"Butt-kisser!" Payaso mumbled, and he and Phatty busted out laughing.

Phatty and Payaso made their plans for the next day and parted ways. "Love ya!" Payaso yelled as he started for the door.

"To the moon!" Phatty yelled out as Payaso walked across the hall to his home.

"And back!" Payaso responded, and they both laughed. Payaso went inside his apartment, and all the cats and Stanley quickly fell fast asleep for the night.

Somewhere deep inside Central Park, high up on the rocks, Crawler perched proudly on his new owner's knee. Crawler enjoyed nights like this—a full moon, cool air, and a brisk spring breeze. He felt alive as he watched animals scurry in the park's darkness below him—mice, rats, feral cats. They feared him, and that fear made him feel more than alive. It made him feel powerful and mighty.

From atop the rocks, Crawler and his new master could watch everything, especially the luxury apartments that overlooked the park. *His* park, Crawler reminded himself. Central Park was his now, and he didn't waste any time making sure that every animal there knew of him and feared him.

Crawler smiled at the warm, long strokes of affection as his owner petted him. He had never been petted like this in the zoo or even at the circus. Nobody had loved him or cared for him. In fact, at the circus, he was just a trained performer; nobody there ever took the time to get to know him. After the ... accident, he'd been discarded like trash. Then, when he didn't think things could get worse, he arrived at the zoo. Immediately the other animals mocked him, mistreated him, and excluded him from any social groups. Animals could be cruel to one another, and he was walking proof of that.

The zookeeper did what he could to help Crawler, separating him into his own cage when the others had pecked him bloody. And when the other animals stole his food, the zookeeper would hand-feed Crawler. Up to that point, the zookeeper was the closest thing to a friend Crawler had ever had, but he still didn't feel like he belonged. Nobody had ever made him feel like he belonged—not until Norman.

After Crawler had broken free from his cage at the zoo, the hawk thought the world would be at his feet. However, Crawler couldn't seem to adapt to killing his own food or making a nest from scratch like the other hawks in the park. Norman had found Crawler sulking, scared, and starving to death.

From a time as far back as he could remember, Crawler's food had been brought to him, served on a silver platter after he finished a trick or imitated what the human trainer had showed him to do. Because the circus and the zoo had always fed Crawler, he had never learned how to hunt. And Crawler had also been given a bed; he didn't have to make one out of trash or leaves and scraps. His bed at the zoo was a slightly worn, albeit fabulous, foam-top mattress made just for him. It was a far cry from the hard, wet, cold ground he encountered when he left the zoo. And although he hated being confined by bars and kept under lock and key, Crawler had no idea that being free also had its own restraints.

As Crawler thought back to those first few weeks on his own, in the dead of winter, with no friends, no family, and nobody to show him how to survive, he shuddered. Had Norman not befriended him, fed him, and given him a home, Crawler was sure he would not have made it to see spring in Central Park. Norman had saved his life, and now he owed his life to Norman.

Norman hummed as he gently stroked Crawler's head with his stained hands. His yellow, rotting teeth frantically ground together as he chewed on his nicotine gum. Wildly and rapidly he muttered his new plans to Crawler, his voice raspy and ugly from years of tobacco abuse. In between crazed whispers of his newfangled plans, Norman inhaled large drags from his cigarette, his hands shaking from the nicotine rush.

"My sweet bird, you are so strong and powerful." Crawler's new owner fussed over the hawk as they sat together on the rocks, his voice a dark whisper. His hands shook violently now as he spoke. Although Crawler owed his life to Norman, he secretly wished Norman would remember the importance of good hygiene, as the smell of Norman's breath almost knocked him out.

"Tomorrow, we'll start the next phase of our plan, and by the end of the week, all the jewelry in that big apartment will be ours. Our plan is flawless. You've done well so far. Tomorrow, it's your job to get those animals out of the house by midday. After the sun sets and it's dark, go through the window and search for the jewelry. Piece by piece you'll fly it down to the corner where I will be waiting, and together we will have everything. It will all be ours, Crawler!"

Crawler's belly warmed, and he tried his best to smile through his mangled beak as he let out a loud and long squawk. This warmth, he could only imagine, must be what love felt like. Nobody had ever included him, let alone cared for him, before Norman. Looking over at Phatty's apartment from the top of the rocks, the rosebush on the balcony swaying in the wind, he felt once again that sensational rush of power.

For the first time in his life, he was not the one who feared but rather the one who caused fear. At the thought of that, excitement pulsed through Crawler's body. His life had finally begun. Before he knew it, the dastardly plan of theirs would be finished, and he would finally have his own happily ever after. Together, he and Norman would see the world, and he would never have to worry about being picked on again.

CHAPTER 5

By six o'clock Wednesday morning, Payaso was up and ready to head over to Phatty's house. His mom knew the routine: he would wake up, wake everyone else up, have his breakfast, and then wait at the door meowing until someone finally unlocked the dead bolt so he could head out for the day. He was a unique cat, to say the least, but while he could open any door he wanted, he had yet to figure out how to unlock a dead bolt. Many a night he had exhausted himself trying, but to no avail. He prided himself on his intelligence, but he got by with his charm.

Payaso's family owned a bookstore, so he had spent hours reading and educating himself. He enjoyed self-help books, learning languages, and reading about places to go. And despite knowing that it would cause a bad dream or two, he even enjoyed reading the occasional thriller.

Payaso also enjoyed listening to his mom talk on the phone. She was so smart, and Payaso loved her so much that every night he slept on the pillow next to her head. He told Phatty that he slept as close to her head as possible, because it not only made him feel safe, but he also thought that some of her "smartness" might rub off on him.

Phatty was at the door waiting for Payaso to arrive, his tail swishing anxiously.

"Buenos dias," purred Payaso as he walked through the door, exuding his normal allure as he announced his arrival in a foreign language. Payaso was eager to start on their big plans for the day. He had spent the night working on booby traps and ways for Phatty to overcome some of his fear of the birds and Crawler. He just needed to show Phatty how to stand up to them. There would be no playing today. Instead, they were going to work on Phatty's confidence—whether Phatty liked it or not.

"¡Hola, mis gran amigos!" exclaimed Payaso. "That means," Payaso added, as usual answering a question that nobody had asked, "'Hello, my great friends' in Spanish." He beamed, waiting to hear how impressed the group was.

"Do you mind, big mouth?" Clyde said, yawning. "I was enjoying a siesta. *Siesta*—yeah, see, I know some Spanish too, but you don't hear me bragging and yelling it all around the place." Clyde thumped his tail in annoyance, hissed, turned his back on the know-it-all, and laid back down.

Phatty skittered about the floor in excitement. "I have a great new toy we can try today," exclaimed Phatty as he wobbled to get it.

"Ningunos juegos hoy," Payaso stated a bit sternly.

"Ummm … I don't know what you just said," exclaimed Phatty with clear unease. "But I already know I won't like it."

"It means 'no games today' in Spanish," explained Payaso. "We, my friend, are going to conquer some of your fears while building some of the best booby traps this side of the M-i-s-s-i-s-s-i-p-p-i!"

"Conquer fears? *C-R-A-P-P!*" said Phatty, attempting to spell *crap*. Stanley and Payaso laughed.

"Nice try," Payaso said, still laughing.

"Okay," Phatty mumbled. "Now I know what it means and I don't like how it sounds in English, either! Can't we just work on the traps?"

"Non, nein, and just plain *no.* It's not just about setting booby traps, Phatty! It's not just about building the traps. It must be about overcoming your fears," said Payaso as he wrote *F-E-A-R* in capital letters in the air with his paw. "I worry that if we don't work on this, you're going to go through life scared of everything and everyone. That is no way to live, Phatty! It just isn't!"

Phatty jumped off his favorite chair, apparently deciding he would much rather hide under the couch until Payaso got over his new idea.

"Now stop being stubborn, Phatty, and come out here! We can make it fun—like a big adventure!" Payaso was now half under the couch, his butt sticking straight up in the air as he tried to pull Phatty out from the familiar hiding spot.

"Oh, great. It's seven a.m., and already the fur ball is giving a lecture," mumbled Clyde. He rose from his surly nap and strode over to Phatty and Payaso. "But at least you're getting smart and talking out of your better side." He giggled and pointed at Payaso's butt.

"Good one, Clyde!" laughed Stanley. His doggie face was split into a mocking grin. His white fur gleamed in the morning sunshine.

Clyde climbed up on the back of the couch for a better view.

Stanley began to circle the room. "Adventures! I love adventures!" he exclaimed. "Did I hear we are going on an adventure? Hey, how do you say 'adventures' in a fancy language, Payaso?"

"Well"—Payaso beamed—"what language would you like?"

"Hmmm, well, my mom says I'm Maltese. Do you know Maltese?" Stanley asked.

"No, not yet," said Payaso, feeling a bit deflated and wondering what *Maltese* even meant.

Hearing this conversation, Phatty came back out from under the couch. "Payaso, did I hear that right? Was there something you didn't know?" he asked.

"Of course, silly. Nobody can know everything. If they did, there would be nothing left to learn, and I love to learn!" said Payaso.

Stanley, still circling the room, exclaimed, "I want to learn! I want to learn too! Teach me the word 'adventure' in Spanish!"

"Aventura," exclaimed Phatty before Payaso could answer.

At once, all the animals looked at Phatty, their mouths open in shock.

"That is correct!" shouted Payaso. "I am so proud of you, my friend! How did you know that?"

"Well, that's simple. I always listen to you," Phatty explained. "Do you think I could learn as much as you?"

Payaso paused just as a horrible thought occurred to him: *What would happen if Phatty learned everything that I know? Would he even want me around anymore? Then maybe I wouldn't be important or needed anymore.* Payaso's heart ached at the horrible thought, and he briefly wondered if teaching Phatty was a mistake. How would he feel if his friend no longer needed him? Maybe it would be better if he stopped teaching Phatty so Phatty would forever have to depend on him.

But as soon as Payaso looked over at his friend, anxious and excited to continue, Payaso knew exactly what he had to do.

"Sure, Phatty," Payaso said, more softly than usual, his heart breaking. "If you wanted, I could teach you anything. We can even learn together."

"No," moped Phatty. "I doubt it. I know I'm not as smart as you. After all, I'm afraid of everything! People, animals, the dark … even the vacuum can make me jump off the terrace. Yesterday, the wind knocked over a frame, and I fell off my chair." Phatty pretended to leap as he exclaimed, "Last week, even a bird outsmarted me, and now here I am thinking about building a booby trap to protect me. How silly is that?"

A bit out of breath, Phatty sighed as he rolled over onto his back and just stared at the ceiling. "We're running out of time anyway. It's already Wednesday morning. We only have till tonight!" He lost his breath again. "And apparently, I'm fat too," he quietly whispered.

"He does have a good point," Clyde chimed in. He stretched his sleek length out and performed a downward-facing dog, a pose his mother imitated sometimes, with unpleasant results. "Not about the fat part—I personally just think he's big-boned. But he does have a good point about the time. We are running out of it. And I have to agree with him about the booby traps. I'd really like to surprise that big, nasty beast. As for the bird outsmarting him, well, let's just say a cat running from a bird is just against the laws of nature!"

"I will have none of this." Payaso stood on his hind legs and walked quickly across the room. "Phatty," he said, "if you learn one thing, let it be that there is no such thing as not being smart enough. I bet that you alone could come up with all the ideas about the booby traps. You can do anything you put your mind to!"

Payaso continued, "The only thing that makes anyone dumb is refusing to learn. And you, my friend, can learn! You remembered; you listened. You can do anything, and even if you can't, you have to try. I believe it was—"

"Here we go," moaned Clyde. He pretended to ignore Payaso and walk toward the door. "Seriously, though, where are you going with all of this?" he muttered quietly.

Payaso ignored Clyde and continued talking, this time even louder. "I believe it was Stephen Kaggwa who said, 'Try and fail, but don't fail to try.' And—"

"So what does that even mean?" interrupted Clyde. "Does that mean that I shouldn't *try* and tumble you to the ground to shut you up right now? Or does that mean that I *should* try, even though I know you will keep on talking either way?" Clyde licked his paws in preparation for a pounce.

"What it means, Mr. Jingle Brains, is that all of us are capable of trying anything. It means you can always learn and should always attempt to live without fear."

He turned to his friend. "Phatty, you need to remember that everyone is born with some unique strength—something that they are great at. You need to find your own strength. Tell me, what are your ideas about the booby trap?"

"I don't know. I have no idea! That is why I asked you," Phatty said.

Payaso looked at him and asked, "Imagine I was still back in Seattle, and I wasn't coming for another month. What would you do?"

Phatty rolled over. "Well, first, I would put clear tape on the edge of all the window frames, so this way if he opened the window, the tape would break and then I could always tell after a nap if anyone had opened a window." Phatty looked around. Everyone seemed very impressed by his idea. He sat up straighter, and his shoulders set with more confidence.

"Well, that sounds easy enough," Stan said. "But that won't stop him."

"Yes, but I like where you are going, Phatty," Payaso chimed in. "You could do something similar with string. You could put a tiny string at the bottom of the doors to the terrace, in the doorjamb, like this." Payaso demonstrated by placing a tiny piece of string in the doorjamb, just enough so it was stuck and hardly visible. "If the door was opened while you were napping, you could tell because the string would fall out, like this." Payaso opened the door, causing the string to fall down.

"Yes, this is all good," Clyde interrupted. "But I hardly think these ideas are going to do the trick. We need something to help catch him or send him on his way."

"I know," Phatty said, with even more confidence showing.

"I think we should also set up something that would startle Crawler—maybe even enough to scare him away or make him think twice. At the same time, the noise will alert us that he was trying to get inside." Phatty beamed with pride at his idea, which grew when he stared at his friend and his brothers, who looked awestruck.

Phatty got up now and began walking around, gesticulating. He elaborately explained his plans to rig items to fall on piano keys should Crawler trigger the trap when opening a window, and the same for the net that would be set up to trap Crawler on the terrace. The net would fall on Crawler the minute he opened the window from either side, guaranteeing that they would catch Crawler on the way in to steal the jewels or on the way out. "Then I would stuff all my toys in the closet where my mom keeps her jewels so that when Crawler opened the closet door, all of the toys would pop out and fall on him. Maybe that would even scare him out of the house!"

Payaso was so excited, he jumped up and started to run in circles. "Great beaver dams! Phatty, that's excellent! You have such amazing ideas, and you never even picked up a book or searched the internet! See how smart you are? I told you. You have so many great qualities that give you so much power that I don't know where to begin!" Running back up to the couch, he exclaimed, "Phatty, my friend, let's start right away!"

Just then, the doorbell rang and interrupted Payaso's speech.

As fast as he could, Phatty ran under the couch to hide, not realizing that only the front half of his body was hidden. His butt, back legs, and tail stuck out. Payaso chuckled at the sight of Phatty.

"I can hear you," hissed Phatty in a low, embarrassed mumble. Phatty still had a lot to learn.

CHAPTER 6

The doorbell turned out to be UPS delivery—the usual assortment of boxes and packages. A couple of hours later, the animals were hard at work, and Phatty was growing tired. Plotting and schemes were exhausting!

"Okay, let's start with the windows and doors," Payaso announced as he emptied the contents of a huge knapsack onto the floor: string, duct tape, a net, a bag filled with ping-pong balls, and even a few confetti poppers.

"Where did you get all of this?" Phatty giggled as he rummaged through the pile and tangled himself up in the big net, trying to nudge one of the balls with his nose.

"My mom's grandkids … wait … hmm, does that make them my cousins? Grandcousins, maybe? Geez, maybe they are not even related to me?" Payaso paused, quizzical, untangling Phatty. "No, they must be related, right? They do have my intelligence, so I would say yes; for sure, they must be related to me—"

"Hey, Hot Cross Butts! Can we zip the family tree history and focus?" Clyde snapped.

Payaso cleared his throat and went on to explain what

he had found on the internet while Stanley stood watch to ensure the birds couldn't see their planning. Clyde agreed with Payaso, clearly impressed with what Payaso found on this so-called "inter-web of knowledge." And Payaso agreed with Clyde, who had pointed out that for every action there was a reaction. This meant that if they managed to catch Crawler off guard, his reaction could be what would help them take him down.

As Phatty watched them doing their tasks, he couldn't believe how well everyone was getting along. Payaso and Clyde hadn't argued once, and they had almost finished one window trap. They worked together to shove balls, toys, and anything they could find into the jewelry cabinet and cat-food pantry. Phatty had insisted that their food be protected at all costs. They toiled together on the window for what felt like hours.

Together, Phatty purred to himself. *We are all working together!* To Phatty, it was the best feeling in the world. Well … the best feeling next to treats.

"How about we tie the string to the window?" Phatty said as he walked in circles. "And then we can connect it to the framed picture sitting on the piano. If the screen is pushed open, the string will tug on the frame, making it fall on the piano keys. That should make a big enough noise that we all hear it!" Phatty was so proud of himself.

"Yep, that's perfect," Payaso said. "Then let's put this trap on the next window." He pointed to the confetti poppers, duct tape, and string, while explaining the role each would play in the contraption. "When he breaks in, first he'll be stunned by the exploding confetti, which will then cause him to take a step back, triggering the net to drop on him from above. If the loud pop of the confetti doesn't scare the heck out of him, the confetti-and-net combination will for sure!"

After a few hours of work, they all felt proud of what they had accomplished. Payaso sighed and lay down on the sun-warmed carpet. "Even I'm getting tired, and I'll bet everyone else is too."

Clyde and Stanley nodded. "Yeah, let's rest," Stanley said and plopped down not far from Payaso.

"How about we clean up now, before we run out of steam?" said Phatty. "We've already finished both windows, the cabinet, the back door, and"—eyeing his stomach with a little sarcasm—"of course the food pantry."

"There is not much more we can do," said Clyde, "and to be honest, I think that's enough to get him, hopefully, or at the very least scare him good!"

Phatty's heart sank a bit. He wished he could be positive that this was enough to stop the hawk. A big yawn came over him, and he headed to his favorite spot under the couch. Halfway under, Phatty felt his eyes get heavy, and as he stretched out, he started to fall asleep.

Payaso looked over to see his only friend's butt sticking out from under the couch, almost like a bear that got stuck in his cave's entryway and couldn't move. Phatty had wedged himself under the furniture in such a way that only his butt, back legs, and tail remained visible. The way his back legs sprawled out under his body forced his butt to stick up.

Payaso couldn't help but giggle at the sight. He loved that Phatty could always make him laugh—even if he wasn't trying to! His heart swelled. He never knew that he could love another animal as much as he loved his best friend. Phatty was the kindest and sweetest friend in the world, and Payaso would do whatever was necessary to protect him.

As Payaso made himself comfortable, he could hear the birds gathering on the small trees and bushes on the apartment terrace. The terrace was adorned with several planters full of shrubs, miniature trees, and colorful plants that bloomed with every season. It was landscaped to make you feel like you were sitting in a park overlooking the park; there was even a fountain and trellises covered in ivy and blooming roses—red, pink, violet. The birds loved the terrace, and many of them chose to build their nests inside some of the large bushes and trees; they believed the terrace was as much their home as it was Phatty's. They gathered now, like they did every early afternoon, to enjoy lunch and take a nap.

The noise on the terrace grew louder as more and more birds arrived and began chuckling from the window ledge at the sight of Phatty's butt sticking out from under the couch. One by one they began to chime in, laughing harder and harder. It bothered Payaso to see anyone laughing at his friend.

"Look at that stupid, fat cat," chirped one of the birds, pointing his wing at Phatty. "Crawler says he drools like a baby and cries like one too!"

"A baby whale maybe!" chirped a bird from another branch. It had a weird splotch of white on its red chest.

"It looks like he ate the couch!" chirped another bird.

They all laughed in unison, continuing on at Phatty's expense.

Payaso grew furious as he listened. He was trying desperately to think of something clever to say back to them, something smart from his books. Suddenly, Payaso caught sight of Clyde crawling below the window where the birds couldn't see him, gliding across the floor with impressive speed and accuracy.

Stanley was watching now too, admiring Clyde's patience as he waited, observing the birds laughing at his shy, overweight brother, preparing to strike at just the right moment, until … Clyde jumped toward the glass! He roared a most ferocious growl—like a lion on the savannah—as the crash of his body against the window sent the birds scattering in every direction.

"Benedict Cumberbatch!" he yelled, and all the birds

frantically collided as they flew away from the terrace, petrified.

Clyde sat proudly at the window, shoulders squared, leisurely licking his paws, sending a silent message to the bullies outside. He glanced over at Payaso. "I hope they will take that message back to Crawler! Score: Clyde 1, Crawler 0!"

Payaso was impressed by Clyde's bravery and desire to protect his brother. It was like a scene from one of Payaso's action-adventure books. But before he could make a comment, Stanley and Clyde were already back to their afternoon naps, and it wasn't long before Payaso was sound asleep too.

Although he had been half under the couch, Phatty *had* been awake and heard the entire bird incident. He was so embarrassed, yet again. He knew the feathered beasts were laughing at him—just like they did every day. And today, to make it worse, it happened in front of his best friend, Payaso.

I am so tired of being a scaredy-cat. Phatty's emotions ranged from anger to sadness to pure infuriation. He felt his heart speed up and then slow.

Quietly, so he didn't awaken his brothers or his friend, Phatty crawled out from under the couch. To his horror, in the large window seat on the other side of the glass sat Crawler.

Phatty forced himself to stay put, driven now by pure rage. He puffed out his chest, sucked in his big belly, and squished his face. He gave Crawler the ugliest, meanest stare anyone had ever seen. Staring steadily at the big mangled mess of a waste of flying species, Phatty drew a deep breath and with all of the courage he had, stormed the window, picking up more and more speed as his paws raced across the floor.

He reached the window ledge and, in one swoop, leaped up onto it, landed with a loud thump, and locked eyes with the mangled beast—for the briefest moment. But the momentum from Phatty's landing was so strong that he started sliding across the window ledge's smooth surface. Screaming madly and sliding faster and faster, Phatty crashed into the window glass. Still, Crawler was clearly so shocked by the sudden and fast movement of a thirty-pound cat hurling himself in attack that he jumped back, squawking and flapping his wings in shock.

At the sight of Crawler retreating, Phatty felt oddly victorious, though pain from the crash began pounding in his head and the room started to spin. For the first time, Phatty didn't run away from a bully but straight toward him. Just as he was basking in the glow of the proudest moment of his life, the spinning in Phatty's head became too much. Phatty toppled backward and, without realizing, slipped off the window seat and fell smack down onto the floor, landing with a heavy and loud *oomph*. He could hear the laughter of the hawk fill the room once again, and it enraged him.

Picking himself up off the floor, Phatty jumped back up onto the window ledge and sat as close to the glass as possible. Though scared deep down, he was ready to show the hawk just who was the boss in this apartment. As Phatty pressed his face to the window, the hawk locked eyes with him once again.

"I am going to come back for your friends, and one by one, they will be mine." The hawk growled and tapped his beak on the window. The golds and browns in his feathers mixed with his creamy underbelly, almost pretty in the afternoon sun.

"Bring it on, Jumpin' Jehoshaphat!" Phatty growled. He slammed his paw as hard as he could on the glass, and to his delight, Crawler was so shocked by Phatty's aggression that the hawk jumped back from the window and flew off.

Phatty felt his legs shaking. His heart raced as he felt victory for the first time. He looked around to see his friends' reactions—and there they were, all sleeping. Nobody had witnessed it!

"Son of a bichon!" Phatty exclaimed. "Sure, everyone

witnesses every other time I have a run-in with birds, but here I am, standing up for myself to the large mouth out there, and nobody sees it!"

He glanced about the room at his friends all napping around him. Right then and there, Phatty knew what he needed to do. He needed to go to the park and stop Crawler. He was no longer going to live in fear in his own home, and he needed a way to prove to everyone that he was brave. This was his moment. This was his time to prove that he could solve his own problems and protect his family.

Phatty saw the laundry bag by the door ready for the pickup laundry service. He knew by how the arrows were positioned on the clock that a human was about to enter the apartment and pick it up. He quickly left a jumbled note to his brothers and Payaso so as not to let his absence worry them.

Then he jumped into the laundry bag and waited, knowing that at any minute he would be whisked outside, where Phatty would make his escape and stop Crawler once and for all.

CHAPTER 7

A few hours later, Clyde awakened from his nap just in time to witness Payaso waltzing back and forth pretending to be him.

"Babaaaaam!" Payaso whispered as he jumped at the window, pretending to scare birds.

"You have to be tougher, Payaso!" exclaimed Stanley. "Go *raaaaahhhh*! Then *babaaaam*, at the same time as you jump toward the window. That's how Clyde did it!"

"Raaaaahhhh!" Clyde yelled from behind, scaring them both silly.

"¡Ay, caramba!" Payaso exclaimed, freezing and dropping onto the carpet like a bag of rocks.

Clyde jumped over to the coffee table where the boys were playing. "You're starting too close to the window, Payaso. You need to add the surprise factor. From where you're standing, they can see you coming," Clyde explained. "FYI, kind of kills the entire art of surprise and all, the birds seeing your furry know-it-all face gawking at them."

Payaso sat down and groomed himself frantically, clearly trying to hide his embarrassment. "Good job being the lookout,

Stan," Payaso mumbled. "You were supposed to let me know if Clyde woke up!"

Stanley went back to his bed to pout. Clyde got up and did a long, lazy stretch, and then he began to search for his brother Phatty.

"Where could he be?" Clyde asked, hoping Stan or Payaso knew. He rambled through the living room, the pantry (a likely choice, usually), the kitchen, even their parents' bedroom. No sign of his brother. Then, checking near their food bowls, Clyde found the note:

> Bouys,
>
> I went to the parck to be brav. Dont be wurid. I wil be gud. The bid berd wuz heer agen to steel and I need to stopp him. Goin 2 the zuu to geht helps.
>
> Luv,
>
> The Phatty

They were all speechless.

Stan was the first to break the silence. "Wow! Phatty is an awful speller!"

"Never mind that," Clyde exclaimed. "He is in the park! Phatty is in the park, *all alone*! We have to go and find him!"

"What will we do?" Payaso yelled, his voice sounding on the edge of panic.

Clyde ran to the living room window to look down at Central Park. "Quick! Come here!" he said to the others. "Can you see him down there?" Stanley sounded hopeful—too hopeful.

"The park is so big," Clyde exclaimed as he strained to see a sign of Phatty anywhere.

"Actually, the park is 840 acres, and today, Central Park is the most visited urban park in the United States ..." mumbled Payaso, unable to help himself.

Clyde glared at Payaso. "I think we need to come up with a plan to go to the park and find him," Clyde said, pausing to gauge the others' expressions. "Phatty may be in a ton of trouble. I say we find him and bring him home before anything bad happens to anyone. And we have to do it before that nasty Crawler finds him!"

Clyde did his best to speak calmly and with certainty, although his voice couldn't hide his fear. He looked at Payaso. "Any bright ideas, Mr. Genius?"

"No," said Payaso in a barely audible voice. "I feel terrible. What have I started? Where is my friend?" He swallowed jumpily, and his eyes misted with tears.

"Please help us, Clyde! How do we get him back?" Stan cried out.

"Stan," said Clyde, "calm down and go get Mommy's running map of Central Park. I think Phatty will head for the big rocks, the ones he watches from the terrace. Plus, that would be the best place for him to watch for Crawler."

Next, Clyde directed Payaso. "Payaso, jump on the counter and push down Stan's leash, then knock off that raincoat from the coat stand. I'll go make sure all the booby traps are set in case Crawler tries to break in while we are gone. Do we all know what we need to do?"

Payaso and Stanley nodded.

Clyde continued, "Okay, let's meet at the door in five minutes. Payaso, when you're done, go grab that ridiculous hat you had on yesterday when you were pretending to be French."

"Oh, I love that French hat ..." Payaso began.

"*Focus,* Payaso!" Clyde growled. "I am not saying to go get that hat because I want a fashion show. We're going to need a disguise if we want to get out of this building without someone calling the ASPCA!"

—·▪■▪·—

Clyde had taken charge. Payaso was in awe, but he quickly began worrying again. *What have I done*? Payaso thought he had failed his best friend, Phatty.

"Don't be sad, Payaso. We will find Phatty," Stanley whispered. He seemed to understand the cat's fear and sadness. "I'm worried too, but trust me, if anyone can find my brother, it's Clyde."

Payaso nodded as he tried to swallow the lump in his throat. He did what Clyde had instructed and ran across the hall to find his French hat. As Payaso got to his door, he looked back.

"To the moon," Payaso yelled to Phatty out of habit. Payaso realized he was staring at an empty doorway, and the tears he had been holding back finally won.

—·▪■▪·—

Five minutes later, they were all at the apartment door.

"What do we do now?" asked Stan.

"Now we're going to dress up like a human and pretend to take you to the park for a walk," Clyde explained, turning to Payaso. "Payaso, please hook up Stan's leash."

Payaso's jaw dropped as he took in Clyde's plan. *Brilliant! It's just brilliant!* Payaso gave Clyde another look of admiration. As Clyde worked his way into the trench coat, Payaso realized he had underestimated the cat.

Clyde turned to Payaso and said, "Put your hat on and get on my shoulders. And try to be dainty about it, will ya?"

Payaso took a deep breath. He climbed up, scrambled into the top part of the raincoat, and flipped up the collar. Then he wiggled about and adjusted the hat so that his entire head was covered. He tucked down his chin so that his entire face was hidden. With Payaso's back paws on Clyde's shoulders, standing as tall as he could, the map of Central Park tucked in the coat pocket and Clyde standing on his hind legs, they carefully turned to face the door. Clyde had left one button on the raincoat undone; it was the one directly in front of his eyes, allowing him to see out without anyone seeing in.

Clyde handed Payaso the leash. Payaso carefully opened the apartment door. The stacked cat duo wibbled and wobbled their way down the hallway to the elevators, Stanley on his leash trotting at their side.

"If I may point out," Stanley blurted, "this is where Payaso's thumbs really come in handy."

Clyde knew Stanley was right, but he didn't want to admit it. He just needed to make sure he could see where he was walking so they didn't fall down on their heads and get discovered. "Let's just focus on not falling," Clyde said. "Payaso, you hit the elevator button. Then, once we're on the elevator, hit the *L* button to go to the lobby."

They stood in silence, teetering and balancing on each other, as they waited for the elevator to arrive at their floor.

"Excuse me, are you implying that I do not know what the *L* button means in the elevator?" asked Payaso, clearly annoyed. "I have been riding elevators my entire life," he continued proudly.

"Payaso," Clyde mumbled. "You weigh a ton."

"Yes," Payaso sniffed proudly. "But the weight is all in my brain."

The elevator arrived, but when it opened, they saw a gray-haired, bespectacled man and his very large dog standing in the far corner. Both cats froze inside the raincoat, afraid the dog would smell them.

"Well, Mister 'I Have Been Riding Elevators My Entire Life,' what does one do when the elevator has a huge dog heading out for its walk on it?" Clyde hissed angrily at Payaso. "If this dog smells us, he'll definitely blow our cover. But then, of course, there is the bigger issue that he will most likely eat us!"

Stan, oblivious to the situation, marched into the elevator like normal. The leash stretched now, pulling taut and causing the feline tower to wobble.

Payaso was still speechless with fear.

"Move it," Stanley whispered to Clyde.

"Move it?" Clyde whispered back. "We'll end up an afternoon snack for this dog! Let's wait for the next elevator!"

"D-d-don't m-m-move," Payaso managed to stutter through gritted teeth.

"There is no time, and what choice do we have? *Hello!* I'm already on the elevator!" Stanley snapped back at them.

"Ahhhhheeem." The man on the elevator cleared his throat. He rolled his eyes to the dog and gestured with his hand for the raincoat tower to either get on or get off the elevator.

The man's dog frantically sniffed at the air, drooling everywhere.

Payaso stared at the panting dog from behind the raincoat's big collar while Clyde peeked out from the tiny opening in the jacket. "For the love of good gumbo!" Payaso gasped, appalled at the amount of drool dripping from the dog's mouth. "Try a breath mint, Kibbles and Bits!"

In reaction to Payaso's comment, the dog bucked wildly on the leash, lunging at them as his jaw snapped wildly at the air.

"Good job, Dick Butkus!" hissed Clyde at Payaso. "Please, poke the raging bear some more!"

"Easy! Easy, boy!" the man yelled at his dog, trying to hold him back, growing impatient at the figure delaying the elevator. "On or off, sirrrrrr … errrr, ma …" Unsure if the figure was male or female, the man stopped himself.

"Backward! Move backward!" Payaso insisted to Clyde. They stumbled backward, trying to pull Stanley off the elevator.

Reversing their awkward raincoat tower, they wobbled back and forth, desperately trying to keep from falling while cautiously watching the drooling hound.

"Woof!" Stanley barked directly in the snarling dog's face. His bark broke the elevator's silence, startling everyone, including Clyde, who hopped backward, twisting his leg, which caused him to slip and lose his balance.

"Whoa, Nelly!" Clyde screamed out as the pair toppled forward, directly into the elevator. Careening forward, the raincoat tower of cats hit the wall with a loud thump.

As they were half slumped now against the elevator wall, their choice had been made for them; they were on the elevator whether they wanted to be or not. They quickly struggled to reestablish their balance. Finally, Clyde straightened up, gaining his composure, while Payaso held his hat in place.

"Moo!" the man yelled at his dog. "Do you see what you just did!" He forced the dog to sit down and tightened his leash. Looking at them, the owner apologized. "I am so sorry! I don't know what has gotten into my dog! Moo is usually a good dog!"

The man in the elevator continued to stare, confused by the tower's silence. He leaned around and tried to see the tower's face. "Sir, err, ahh, if I may." He cleared his throat. "You do realize it is very sunny today? No rain is expected."

The man leaned back, waiting for a response. Curious, he reached out to tap the stranger on the shoulder, but his dog sprang up toward the brim of Payaso's hat, his jaws again violently chomping at the air. The man was forced to pull the dog back in one rapid swoop, and the swift, hard motion had the dog's jowls snapping, covering everyone in the elevator with dog saliva.

"I'm sorry," the man said, embarrassed now as he wiped

Moo's spit off his face. "I don't know what has gotten into him. Moo loves people! He only acts this crazy when he's around cats!"

The elevator thumped to a stop, and the doors finally opened. In unison, Clyde and Payaso expelled a long breath of relief.

The man apologized again before exiting. "Good day," he mumbled as he violently dragged the furious dog off the elevator.

Clyde didn't move.

Stanley looked up and saw that the raincoat was covered in the dog's saliva. "Well, it looks like rain after all!" he laughed. "Come on, what are you waiting for?" He started to walk, pulling on the leash. "Come on!"

Stanley began moving forward but turned around and peered back at the raincoat. Both cats stood still, their eyes shut in fear of the dog.

"Look at you two!" Stanley giggled. "You act as if you've never been around a dog, for crying out loud! He was just playing with you guys. And come on! I would have stopped him before he ate you."

"What?" Payaso and Clyde simultaneously exclaimed, eyes bolting open.

"That dog was a hundred pounds bigger than you, Stanley!" Payaso shrieked. "How were *you* going to stop him? Jump into his mouth before he ate one of us?"

Clyde blurted out, "Yeah, Payaso is right! What were *you* going to do?"

Stanley shushed them both as the elevator door started to close. "Let's go!"

"Who names their dog 'Moo' anyway?" snapped Payaso. "It's a dog, not a darn cow!"

"Looked big enough to be a cow to me!" Clyde mumbled, and Payaso nodded in agreement. They both started laughing—and then stopped when they realized they were not only agreeing but also enjoying each other's company. Neither one was willing to admit that they were more alike than they had realized.

Payaso and Clyde wobbled out into the openness of the building's grand art deco lobby. Payaso touched his paw to his hat and, realizing that he was soaking wet with drool, let out a shriek. "Son of a Bieber! I am covered in dog spit!" he moaned.

"Stan, ignore Holly Golightly above me, and you lead the way. I trust you more than anyone. You do this every day," Clyde directed.

"Go straight. Your first turn's going to be a left. I'll tell you when," Stanley whispered.

As drool dripped down his favorite hat onto his fur, Payaso silently plotted his revenge on that foaming jerk of a beast called Moo.

"Right! Make a right!" Stan yelled.

"But you just said left a minute ago!" Clyde argued.

"Dogs!" Payaso and Clyde said in unison, both realizing they had just agreed on something for the second time that day.

CHAPTER 8

Max Brower balanced his stack of quarters on the back of his hand perfectly while he stood in the lobby of his building debating how he would spend his allowance once inside the park: ice cream, hot dog, or pretzel. He was almost through the fourth grade, and summer couldn't come quickly enough. Today he'd only had a half day of school, which made him long even more for those hot, long, lazy days of July and August when he spent hours exploring the park. The less time at school, the better! Not because he didn't love his teachers or learning, but because he had a tough time making friends with the other kids.

Max was "very special"—at least that's what he overhead the teachers and doctors say sometimes. He knew *special* actually meant *different,* and he was okay with that. What he wasn't okay with was how the other kids made him feel. It was bad enough that Max had flaming-red hair and snow-white skin, with long, lean, gangly legs that knocked when he ran. Max wasn't great in sports; he couldn't act or sing; he couldn't draw or paint. Come to think of it, Max didn't have one talent that made him stand out—aside from his ability to hear and see things very differently from anyone else in his class.

While others saw another kid crying as an opportunity to tease that classmate, Max always saw an opportunity to offer help or just listen. Others would see a spider or bug in the classroom and rush to kill it, while Max would help save the insect—or arachnid—and resettle it back into nature. Max couldn't always use words to express what he wanted or thought, but to his credit, in his own unique way, he always figured out how to communicate through his actions. To express love and kindness, he would offer a hug. To express his interest in getting to know someone, he would offer a wave or flash his smile. He seldom spoke at home, let alone at school or on the playground, where he was the most intimidated. Unfortunately, other kids found his actions off-putting, and his lack of conversation despite warm smiles and waves confused them.

But today, Max was happily focused on his upcoming afternoon in Central Park—until he was suddenly jarred from his thoughts by the strangest sight.

Max wasn't sure what caught his attention first—the little white dog dragging a blob behind him, or the whiskers that stuck out from the collar of the slimy raincoat. The white dog was cute; he couldn't deny that. The pooch's happy expression was mesmerizing. Max gazed at the strange creature holding the dog's leash, and as he looked closer, Max could almost make out the face of a cat under the brim of the hat.

The sound of the bustling blob as it struggled along, dragging a big piece of raincoat behind it, caught the doorman's attention now too. Max didn't know what exactly was going on, but it was clear to him that the cat was trying to disguise itself.

"H-hey, R-richie!" Max blurted out as the doorman pointed at the trench coat–clad figure, moving out of his chair to stop it.

The raincoat person froze now, almost at the entrance of

the building. Richie, the doorman, turned to Max, a look of surprise on his face. In fact, it was actually the first time Max had ever spoken to Richie, who probably hadn't been sure Max could even speak until this very moment.

A cat gazed back at Max from under the too-large hat. Their gazes locked on each other, and then Max gave him a wink and his signature friendly and warm smile.

"A-fter y-you, s-sir," Max said quietly as he extended his arm, allowing the animals to pass.

The raincoat tower stopped and wobbled a bit, and then quickly scuffled forward. All three animals immediately knew that Max was onto them, and they were both shocked and pleased that he had been kind enough to offer a distraction as they scuffled by. Max turned to Richie and quietly asked him about the white dog.

"Oh, that dog? That was Stanley. He lives on the nineteenth floor," Richie answered. Before he could say anything else, Max turned and ran out the front door after them.

—▪■■■▪—

Crossing the always busy and bustling Central Park West was harder than the animals could have ever envisioned. It wasn't just cars the wobbling tower had to watch out for; there were also delivery trucks, rickshaws, bikes, scooters, and a mixture of tourists heading into the park and locals going about their day. Unable to see if any cars were coming, they teetered on the corner for a few moments. Then, to Stanley's joy, he saw his friend Melvin, the bulldog, out for his afternoon walk.

"Nobody move until I say move. I am going to get us across the street with my friend Melvin. He is cool. He won't blow our cover," Stanley assured them.

"Great Gatsby!" Payaso moaned. "Another dog."

Melvin and his owner walked to the corner. His owner

greeted Stanley with a warm, "Hey, Mr. Stanley!" He reached down with his rubber-gloved hands and patted Stanley on the head. Stanley played the part of a dog out for his walk perfectly, accepting the love and reciprocating by rubbing on the man's legs—all while he eyeballed Melvin, who was beginning to sniff the coat. Melvin snorted like a bull and gazed up suspiciously at the raincoat tower.

He was just about to bark at the disguised cats when his owner, who was also staring suspiciously at the tall tower attached to Stanley's dog leash, politely introduced himself. "Um, hi, Stretch. I'm Mike. This is Melvin, my dog. He and Stan are friends. I haven't seen you walking Stanley before …" He continued to eye the tall and suspicious tower. "Is it going to rain?" Mike asked and then looked up at the perfectly blue and sunny sky. Melvin let out a low growl.

"Melvin," Stanley mumbled as he rolled his eyes backward. "Don't jinx my sphinx and ba-ba-rum my cover, if you get my crikey."

"Bah-Hang-Ten, buddy. None of my Bolshevik! If playing with cats in the park is your thing, then Walla Walla Bing Bang, buddy," Melvin answered back in the cryptic code. He snorted again and sent some spittle onto the raincoat, to Payaso's dismay. What was with this spitting thing and dogs anyway?

Payaso and Clyde were stunned silent, unable to make sense of anything the dogs were saying to each other and incapable of imagining why anyone would wear rubber gloves to the park unless planning a murder. Melvin the dog walked quietly and carefully across the street with the strange man, and the raincoat blob followed. Payaso and Clyde didn't say anything about the foreign-speaking dog and Stanley—realizing that, up until now, they had completely underestimated both canines.

Melvin's owner's cell phone rang, interrupting the silence and distracting him from the many questions he had been forming regarding the creepy, furry-faced tower. "Pardon me, this is my agent," he said. "I have to take it."

Stanley had never been more relieved to see a human take a phone call. A few moments later, the animals were across the street and inside the walls of Central Park. Melvin and his rubber-gloved owner parted ways with Stanley and the others.

"What's with the gloved man and the dog from outer space?" Clyde blurted out as if it were burning his lips to keep it in.

"Oh, you mean Melvin? We have our own language on the streets. It's just our way to communicate." Stan looked around to gauge where they should go next.

"And the man walking him, wearing the rubber 'I'm a killer' gloves?" Payaso asked, just as curious as Clyde.

"Oh, he's just an actor," Stanley answered.

"Ahh. I see," both cats murmured, as if Stanley's answer made perfect sense.

"So in exactly which restaurant around here does he work?" Clyde asked, and they all giggled.

Payaso's paw pointed out through the open buttonhole in his jacket to an old large stone shed hidden to the right behind the bushes. "Let's put our clothing in there." At first, Stanley and Clyde refused to move. "Not to worry," exclaimed Payaso. "I know the park well, really."

Stanley and Clyde shrugged and reluctantly agreed to follow Payaso's directions. The tower wobbled down the path and walked into the old stone building.

Once inside the dark structure, Payaso threw off his hat and removed the top half of the raincoat. From there, he jumped down off Clyde's shoulders and dragged the raincoat and hat to the corner of the shed. Clyde stretched and shot a scathing look at Payaso as he rubbed his lower back with his paws. They quickly got out the Central Park map from the raincoat's pocket and looked around at the dark shed.

"Cats can see pretty great in the dark, Stan. Can dogs see

at all?" Clyde asked his brother as he looked around at the cobwebs hanging from the corners of the room and the piles of dirt and dust that covered the floor. The smell of something rotting or something very old was overwhelming.

"I can see the dirt and the bugs and the spiderwebs, if that is what you're asking me," Stanley answered. "What is this place? I have been to the park every day for eight years but I've never seen this before."

Normally, Payaso would jump at the chance to give a history lesson, but now all he cared about was finding his friend. "It's an old fort from when the park was built. They use it now as a lawn shed."

"Really? Well, tie me down and tickle me Elmo! That's your response … 'It's an old fort'?" Clyde asked. "No twenty-minute lecture from Professor 'I Know It All' Payaso?"

Payaso was too focused on the map to respond.

Stanley could hear someone coming down the gravel path. He let out a low growl.

Then the door opened. It was Max.

CHAPTER 9

"Hello?" Max said softly, slowly rocking back and forth. "Hellllooo," he said again, this time even softer and slower, so as not to scare them.

Payaso whispered, "Nobody move, and nobody say a word."

Clyde yelled, "Get him, Stan!"

Stan instinctively started to bark, but he quickly stopped. His barks echoed in the old building.

"Um, excuse me, 'get him'?" Stanley asked. "How exactly do you mean 'get him'? I am only about seven …" Everyone stared at him, their expressions saying everything. "Okay, about eight pounds. But come on, Clyde! I am not a Rottweiler!"

"Get me?" Max questioned, rocking faster.

Then suddenly they heard a loud squawk, and the door slammed shut. Everyone let out a scream. Max jumped quickly for the doorknob, but it was too late.

Max tried the door again. It wouldn't budge. When he peered through the old-fashioned keyhole, he couldn't see light. "I can't see out!" Max said frantically. "The key is still in the door, but on the outside!" Max turned to look at the others, his constant rocking going faster and faster.

"Well, this is awkward," Payaso said. "Locked in a dark room with a stranger. This could go terribly wrong, boys. Terribly wrong."

For a few seconds, nobody spoke. Only light shining in from the two-inch gap under the old wooden door and the stray bits of sun that slipped through the shed's dirty windows—which were covered by overgrown trees—kept them all from total darkness.

"Who is he?" Clyde asked.

"How would I know?" Payaso answered in a loud whisper. "I live here two months of the year!"

"Who am *I*?" Max said.

"Oh, wow, he doesn't even know who he is," Payaso whispered. "See, I told you, this could be very bad."

"Do you think he knows us?" Stanley asked. "I saw him in the lobby."

"If he doesn't know who he is, then how would he know who we are?" Clyde snapped.

"How would I know you?" Max asked.

"Oh, this is bad," Payaso said.

"He doesn't seem to know who anyone is," Stanley said.

"I know who I am! My name is Max," Max answered. His rocking finally began to slow.

"Was he answering me?" Stanley whispered.

"Yes," Max whispered back.

"Hold up," Payaso said. He could hear Clyde's breathing in the dark. "First of all, Clyde, jeez Louise! Why are you breathing so hard? It sounds like you are going to have a heart attack any second! It's like being trapped in here with a brushtail possum!"

Payaso looked around for Clyde, who mouthed the words *brushtail possum* with his paws raised to the sky. "Oh, I don't know!" Clyde blurted out. "Let me see, how about that I am in the dark, I'm locked in a room with you—there's a gift that keeps on giving! And how about the fact that my brother is lost in the park! And then let's not forget there is a stranger in here with us who apparently can not only hear us talking but understand us! And you have the flapjacks to ask me why I am breathing so hard? Or no, wait, let me word it like Mr. Fancypants. Why am I breathing *like a brushtail possum*? As if everyone knows what in the world that even is!"

Clyde's eruption of shouting was followed by total silence as the animals took in the gravity of their situation. Peering through the dark, they all searched one another's expressions to see if they were in agreement that this boy could really hear what they were saying.

"What is a brushtail possum, Payaso?" Stanley innocently asked, finally breaking the silence.

They all began talking all at once, arguing and droning on and on, expressing their anxieties and opinions. Their voices echoed loudly off the walls.

"*Quiet!* Quiet! Please! Everybody calm down!" Max finally blurted out. He flapped his hands around his ears. "I'm Max. I live in your building, and I recognized Stanley from his daily walks." He went on to explain that he had decided to follow Stanley out of the building to see if he needed help. "I am not here to hurt you. I love all animals," he continued while slowly rocking.

"Great, he loves 'all' animals. Clearly he is not smart enough to admit that cats are the only stunning creatures," Payaso chimed in.

"Ask him if can hear what we are thinking too," Stanley whispered to Payaso.

"Of course he can't ..." Clyde paused in curiosity. "You can't hear our thoughts, can you?" he asked Max.

"Of course not!" Max giggled, and then they all laughed. "Let's see how we can get out of this place while all of you tell me who just locked us in and what the heck is going on!" he finally said.

"Where do we start?" Stanley asked, looking at the cats for ideas.

Payaso began. "About eight years ago, I was a kitten then, and I knocked on—"

"Stop!" Clyde interrupted. "He doesn't mean that far back. Let me give you the abbreviated version. The small birds and a crazy hawk pick on my brother. He got upset yesterday when the hawk—who goes by Crawler—threatened to eat my brother and us, blah blah blah, and then he said something about breaking in. We set up hawk traps and thought that would be the end of it, but Phatty snuck out after some birds upset him again today. He left us a note that he is in the park, searching for the zoo to tell someone there to come get Crawler. There it is. So here we are, in the park with this nitwit"—he pointed at Payaso—"who told my brother he could be brave and handle anything and blah, blah, blah … and now we are hoping to find him and just bring him home before Crawler gets in the house or, worse, our parents get home from work."

Max's jaw dropped open. He said nothing, just looked at them with a shocked expression.

"He's got the point of the situation, Clyde," Payaso responded. "Phatty is my best friend. I would be forever grateful if you could help us find him."

"Of course," Max said, and then he whispered, "Let's focus on getting out of this place first, shall we?"

The cats and Stan nodded in agreement and then checked the windows, but none even budged. Years of caked-on dirt had sealed them shut. Stanley crept around the corners of the floor looking for other exits as Max continued working on the front door.

The light that shined through the bottom of the door looked brilliant and bright compared to the vast darkness around them.

"We need that key," Max said as he assessed the situation. "The same key opens the lock from either side. My guess is that these old doors have been here for well over a hundred years. Not much about this shed has been updated, because they're not used for the public, only for storing park items like shovels and lawn equipment."

The animals turned to watch Max pacing. Payaso assumed the human was making mental calculations; he was certainly mumbling to himself the steps to a possible plan.

Finally, Max stopped pacing. "I got it!" He rocked with excitement.

"What exactly do you 'got'?" asked Clyde.

"Kid, your rocking is making me seasick. Do you think you can slow it down a bit?" Payaso asked.

"I … well … I … well, I rock sometimes when I'm nervous. I don't even notice sometimes. It just happens." Max looked down and his face flushed with embarrassment. "I wish I didn't, but I can't seem to stop it … and …" Max stopped rocking with clear effort and changed the subject. "I need something thin and pencil-like. And then I am going to need a sheet of paper or cardboard."

"Oh, this can't be good. He's drafting up a letter for the people who find our bodies!" Payaso shrieked as he put his paw to his head.

Stan and Clyde froze. They both stared at Payaso and then at Max.

Squinting in the dim light, Max gazed at Payaso and smiled at the sight of him preparing for his last moments as if nobody was ever going to open this shed to mow the lawn again. "Is he always this dramatic?" Max asked the group.

"Ha!" Clyde responded. "This is nothing. Wait—just you wait. He's only warming up!"

Max laughed. "What's your name?" he asked Clyde.

Clyde introduced himself, and then he introduced the entire group.

"I know how to get that key on this side of the door. Just find me what I need, and I will be all set." Max watched the group smile with relief and scurry to find paper.

Payaso thought Max looked like he was part of a team—that he belonged. He had only just joined this wacky group, and he was already in the thick of it.

The group quickly found what Max needed: a thin metal rod and the map of the park. They couldn't imagine how these two items would get them out, but they handed both over without further question.

"First, I am going to put the map under the door, and then—"

"He's going to use the metal rod to push the key out of the keyhole on the opposite side," Clyde said, then cleared his throat. "And if we're lucky, the key will land on the map so he can slide the paper and key back under the door, and then he can unlock the door from this side!" Clyde was almost shouting with excitement as he figured out Max's plan. "You're a genius! You're an absolute, hands-down genius!"

"Shama lama ding dong!" Stanley barked out.

Max looked down, the darkness covering his blush—unless, of course, you were a cat and could see in the dark. Payaso grinned.

"Thank you," Max mumbled. "Nobody has ever called me a genius before. I sure hope this works!"

CHAPTER 10

Max slid the paper map a few inches under the door where he believed—well, *hoped*—the key would drop. Stanley and Payaso pressed their heads near the opening under the door to see outside. Max then placed the rod in the lock until he felt it make contact with the key. Carefully and slowly, Max nudged the key forward, trying not to push too hard, hopeful it wouldn't land beyond the map's reach on the ground.

"Okay, here it goes," Max whispered as he nudged the key. "Cross your paws, boys!"

They heard the key clink as it hit the ground, and again as it bounced.

"It's on the paper!" Stanley yelled, wagging his tail in delight. All of them expelled their breath in a sigh of relief.

"Holy Moholy-Nagy!" Clyde whooped out in excitement.

Max quickly peeked under the door for himself. There was the key, half on the paper, half on the ground. Gently, he pulled the paper toward him. Max held his breath as he slowly moved the map, with the key dangling on the end, vibrating as the paper slid across the old dirt floor.

"You're so close!" Stanley squealed.

"We're going to die in here! We'll starve! Someone will one day find our skeletons in here!" wailed Payaso, his normal cool and calm composure just plain gone. He dramatically threw himself on his back and looked up at the ceiling of the dark and filthy shed. His dramatic dive to the ground sent whirlwinds of dirt in every direction. He choked on the dust and then let out a deep and very audible sigh, followed by an even more dramatic gasp.

"We'll be left with the choice of whom to eat first!" Payaso moaned loudly. "We'll be forced to draw straws and then ..." He was almost screaming now as he threw his paws over his filthy face as if he couldn't bear the thought another second.

The group turned and yelled in unison, "Payaso!"

"You're right!" Payaso howled. "Straws? What was I thinking; we don't even *have* straws!" In Payaso's panic, he had missed the entire point. "What a waste my genius brain will be! Oh, and my fur, my stunning fur! I can't be eaten by fellow animals, or worse, starve to death in a work shed in Central Park! It would be like burning a Picasso or smashing a Michelangelo," he said in panic. He jumped to his feet, now throwing his paws toward the ceiling as he paced back and forth on his hind legs.

"Modest one, huh?" Max asked Clyde. Clyde was watching Payaso's meltdown in utter amazement.

"Oh, yes, as modest as they come!" Clyde answered with sarcasm. "Payaso, perhaps if you spent more time trying to figure out how to get us out of here than how the world couldn't go on without you, it would be a bit more useful. After all, you are the genius here. Unless you want to continue your pity party—and if so, please do so without speaking out loud!"

"Woo-hoo! I got it!" Max was smiling from ear to ear as he pulled the key all the way under the door and safely into his hands. They all cheered and clapped. Max swelled with pride.

Even Payaso let out a shout of joy that Clyde thought could

be heard around the park. "I knew you could do it, Max!" Payaso cheered. "Didn't doubt you for one second!"

Max put the key in the lock and turned it. They were all so silent that they could hear the unmistakable click of the door unlocking. Max threw open the door, and they all raced out, toppling over one another on the way.

Payaso was the first one out the door. His feet didn't even touch the ground as he tore out of the shed, his fur flying wildly in the wind as he sprinted to the grass, where he dropped to his knees. Then, while inhaling deep breaths of air, he dramatically gasped, "Great gods of thunder! Feel the grass—it feels like velvet. And the air, smell it!" he exclaimed as he drew in a deep breath. "It's somehow sweeter than before!"

Payaso rolled around taking deep breaths and dramatically screaming praises to the sky, and at anyone who would listen. He looked ridiculous, but Max couldn't help but smile.

Clyde cleared his throat and then spoke sternly. "We can't waste any more time." He looked up at the sky and then continued, "Keep an eye out for Crawler. He may be watching to see if we made it out. Let's just hope he has not found Phatty yet."

Clyde turned to his left and started walking. "This way, everyone. Follow me!"

Payaso jumped up, blades of grass covering his head and his fur as he gazed at Clyde. "Clyde, um, I hate to say this, but … you are going in the wrong direction," he said gently. Pointing in the opposite direction, Payaso explained, "I think Phatty most likely ran toward those big rocks—the ones you can see from your terrace. I imagine they have the best view of where Crawler lives too."

"How do you know what the right direction is, smarty cat? You 'only live here two months of the year.' And since when do you come to the park?" snarled Clyde.

"Well … My mom takes me to the park …" Payaso said very softly.

They all stared at him.

"On a leash?" Max asked, rocking slowly.

"… in a stroller," Payaso mumbled, barely audible.

Clyde snorted, looking at Payaso in disbelief. "Did he just say he comes to the park in a baby stroller?" Clyde turned to Stanley and Max. "Did I just hear that correctly? What self-respecting cat willingly gets into a stroller?"

Max muffled a laugh. The thought of a cat in a stroller struck him as funny too, but he felt bad laughing about it. "Hey, it's cool." Max threw his hands up. "Sounds like your mom is pretty hip. Show us the way, Big P!"

"Well, despite my disdain for Payaso's embarrassing method of transportation, I have to say, I trust Payaso is right," Clyde said. He marched by Payaso and Stanley with his head held high.

Payaso thought about his dear friend alone in the park. Tears welled up in his eyes. Trying not to cry in front of everyone, he walked ahead, holding back the tears with each proud step.

CHAPTER 11

Deep inside the park, Phatty was wondering how he had gotten so lost so fast! Aside from the shrieking of the Asian laundryman who had opened the bag only to find Phatty inside, Phatty had heard nothing else as he jumped out of the bag and made a crazy, wobbling beeline for the park, running as fast and as hard as he could without looking back.

When Phatty finally stopped running, he realized he didn't know where he was. He hadn't thought *this* part of the plan through. From his terrace, Phatty could see clear paths and a tall pile of rocks. From up there, they had looked so easy to navigate. Now, on the ground, the park looked so vast and so complicated.

Around him, humans jogged, walked, strutted, and stumbled by. Phatty had to constantly dodge feet; people clearly weren't paying the least bit of attention to a cat. Dogs on leashes strolled by as well, and some small breeds were actually in strollers—he could hardly believe it—being wheeled about by their humans. Paper trash and garbage lay near the trash bins. Ferns nestled beneath trees and shrubs. Flowers bloomed, sending exotic smells to him, and Phatty distractedly sniffed some daisies. They smelled enchanting.

Phatty looked around, trying to decide where and how to find the rocks. If he could climb to the top of the rocks, he could see well. And he knew the tops of the rocks were visible from the terrace, so there he would somehow leave a message for his friends to read from all the way back home saying that he was okay.

As he walked along looking for the rocks, Phatty quickly grew concerned that maybe he had made a big mistake leaving the safety of his apartment all by himself. There were signs and maps of the park, but they didn't make sense to him. He searched for any path that might take him toward the rocks. Just as he began to feel hopeless, he found one!

Turning down the gravel path, Phatty couldn't help but jump and all but shriek at every strange noise he heard. To calm himself, he tried to focus on the pretty noises, like the wind blowing through the tall green trees or the happy sound of the kids laughing in the playground. He noticed other animals going about their day, and after a while, he started to take comfort in watching them. They didn't look scared to be in the park. He watched a chipmunk scurry through the grass and dogs like his brother out on their afternoon walks. Squirrels scampered up and down trees, chittering, nibbling, tails twitching.

And, of course, Phatty saw lots of birds.

Birds!

"Cheese on crackers!" Phatty called out in frustration as he thought about those pesky, no-good, bullying, flying saddlebags with wings! *The birds and that stupid hawk are what got me into this mess! For years, those mean birds have been taunting and teasing me from the terrace—and then that nasty winged maniac caused this chaos!*

Why in the world were birds of all kind always so mean

to him? Why? It just made no sense to him. He never bothered anyone—especially a bird, that's for dang sure.

But the birds he now watched in the park—cardinals, pigeons, doves, jays, and sparrows—were gathering food and chirping chipperly. They seemed different from the birds that picked on him; these birds didn't even scare him. They didn't even seem to mind him, let alone want to mess with him. Maybe all birds weren't the same? He knew not all dogs and cats were the same. Maybe the birds on his terrace were just nasty, no-good, chucklehead birds?

Focusing now on his path and his plan, Phatty reminded himself that at any moment, Crawler could swoop down or rally those nasty little-beaked big-mouth birds to come after him. He remembered that as sweet as those other birds might look now, chirping and building nests, even those little birds, together in a group, could be vicious.

Phatty's legs began to shake from exhaustion, but he forced himself to keep moving. *Just get to the rocks,* Phatty kept chanting to himself. *First things first: let your family and friends know that you are okay.* He felt silly talking to himself, but he was doing what he could to keep himself focused and calm, and it seemed to be working.

Just when he decided that he couldn't go another step without taking a rest, he saw the rocks. He was almost certain they were the ones he could see from the terrace. He overcame his exhaustion and picked up his pace now, his big belly swinging on the ground, collecting dust, as he jogged on. He tried to remember the last time he had walked fast, let alone run, and smiled at himself for being in better shape than he had given himself credit for. He promised himself that if he made it home okay, he would exercise more and eat a little less ... well, maybe.

When Phatty arrived, he looked up at the top of the rocks, and his jaw dropped. The rocks jutted in and out. They were the color of coal and so shiny that the sun reflected off them.

Phatty reached out with his paw to see if the rocks were as smooth and slick as they looked. The heat burned Phatty's pad, and he quickly withdrew his paw, astonished by the warmth. The rocks were smooth and slippery from years of people climbing. And what upset him the most was that they were a *lot* taller than he had ever realized. It would take all of his energy to climb those rocks, and he would need to be careful to balance his weight as he jumped from ledge to ledge. He swallowed his fear of slipping and focused.

Phatty carefully jumped to the first ledge. His landing was a bit harder than he wanted, and his tiny face hit the rocks in front of him as he skidded clumsily to a stop. Dazed, Phatty shook his head to fix his blurry vision. Carefully now, he leaned onto the next rock and then—slower and a bit more gracefully this time—Phatty leaped up. Winded, he applauded himself for his graceful landing, and he took a second to catch his breath. He looked up again, and the sight of all the rocks still ahead of him was like a blow to his gut. Doubt slowly started to creep into Phatty's mind. This time, for the first time, he swatted it away.

Five more rocks to the top. You can do this.

He jumped again, and his back legs slipped from the ledge. He kicked them out frantically, searching for a grip on any piece of rock for leverage. Imagining what he must look like from below as his butt swung back and forth like a flag in the wind gave him the strength to continue.

Just don't look down! Don't look down. But then he looked down.

"Sweet baby buttercream!" Phatty yelled out loud. "Oh, why did you just look down?!" He was already so high—probably at least four stories. He knew he couldn't survive a fall from this height. His stomach started to feel queasy. *Just focus.* Phatty forced his legs to slow down, and he felt around, finally finding a piece of rock for leverage. Immediately, Phatty used this leverage to jump up to the next ledge, and then, without pausing, he leaped up the last two rocks, propelled by the sheer adrenaline that pumped through him.

When he reached the top, Phatty jumped high in the air, threw his paws up, and screamed at the top of his lungs, "I'll be Jimmy-Jammed!"

Feeling lonesome, he looked up, and way off in the distance, he could see his terrace! The lovely roses on the trellis were visible, and the palms waved in the breeze. Phatty waved, imagining his friends sitting on the terrace looking for him. *Would they believe it was me?*

He was unsure if *he* would even believe it was him if he were not here, panting and a hot mess. Despite being covered in dirt, Phatty wished they could see him now, standing on top of the rocks like a king. Unable to contain his excitement, he shook his hips to the left and to the right while spinning and singing, "Give me a cake! Give me a cake! I'm the best, and I deserve some cake!"

"Pssst. Slim, I hate to interrupt you in the middle of your line dance, but if you're not going to eat that banana, could you toss it my way before you crush my lunch?" a thick, raspy voice asked.

Phatty jumped with fright. A pair of beady eyes peered out at him from between two big rocks!

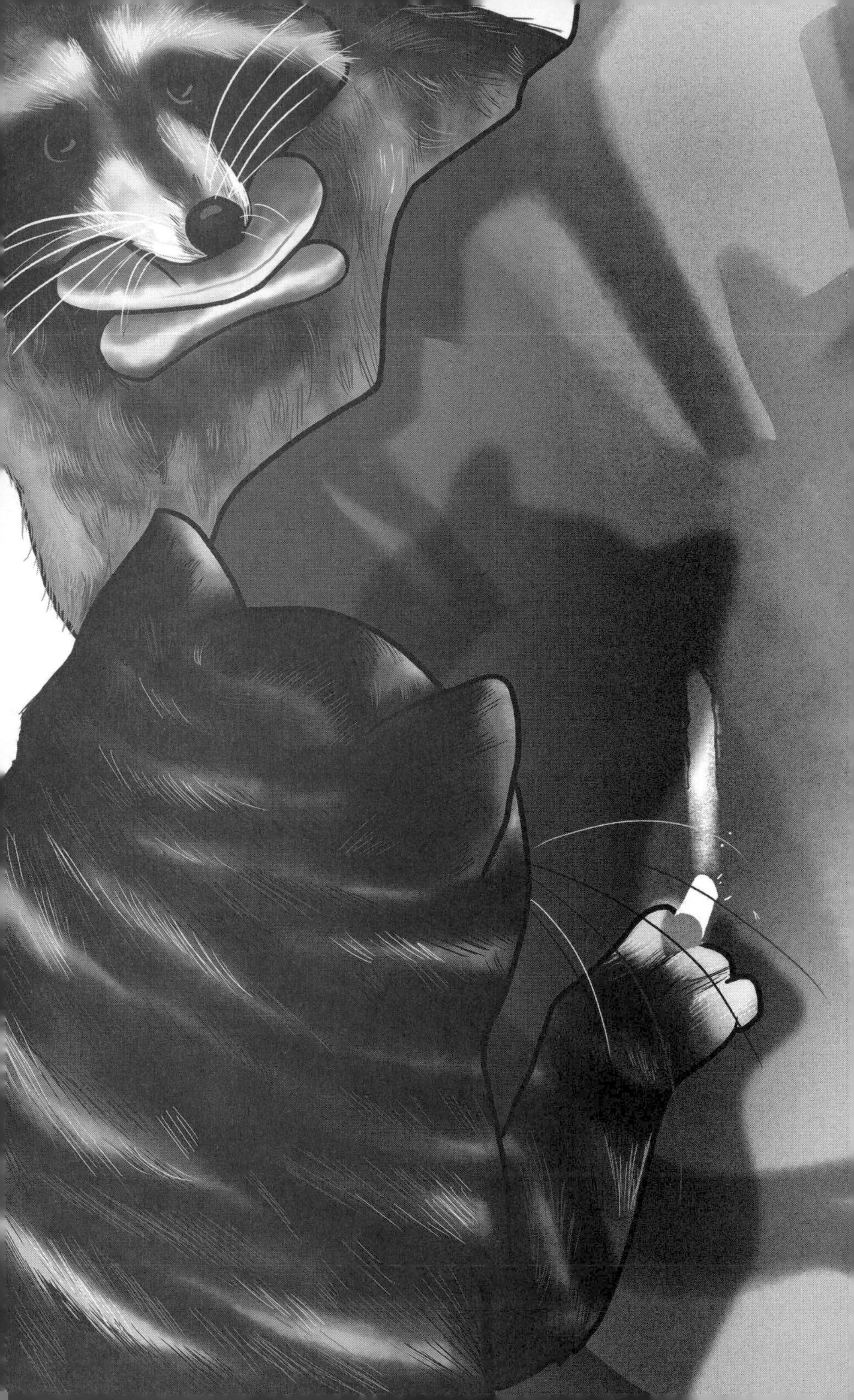

CHAPTER 12

"Eat what?" Phatty exclaimed shakily. His heart was racing, full of fear and also exhausted from the dancing and rock climbing.

"That banana at your feet. Some kids just left it there, and I was hoping to snatch it up just before you came barreling up the rocks and started dancing. In fact, your paws are about to crush it, so if you don't mind, toss it this way, sweet baby buttercream." The raspy voice drew closer, and then in an instant the creature attached to it popped up from behind the rocks.

It was as large as Phatty was, with a black mask over its eyes; gray, ratty-looking fur; and best of all—they were amazing really—tiny hands like a human! They were black with delicate fingers, and they even had tiny fingernails/claws.

Why, it was a raccoon! An animal Phatty had always heard about but had never seen. *It's just a raccoon,* Phatty told himself, trying to remain composed. *Midsize,* Phatty thought to himself. Okay, so he was about the same size as the raccoon. He wondered if that made him a midsize cat? *Focus!*

Carefully, so he didn't squish the brownish, half-rotten,

half-eaten, and disgusting banana, he nudged it toward the raccoon. Phatty was new at this, but he quickly decided that introducing himself might be the best way to go. "I'm-m P-phatty," he stammered, perturbed that his voice shook with fear.

The raccoon said nothing.

Phatty waited for an answer, but nothing came. He watched as the raccoon stretched out its little hand, so humanlike it was alarming, and grabbed the banana just like Phatty's mom would—well, with a nonrotten, non-stranger-mangled banana.

The raccoon peeled the fruit. Holding the rotten, slimy, peeled banana out in its filthy hand, the raccoon rasped, "You want a bite, buttercream?"

Phatty shook his head, too stunned to speak as the raccoon took a large and ravenous bite of the banana. Phatty jumped back when he saw the raccoon's teeth.

The raccoon looked up and smiled. Banana was stuck to most of its teeth, and Phatty was grossed out at the sight. But as manners mattered to Phatty, he did his best to remain polite and expressionless.

"You're jumping back from me?" the raccoon chuckled, its voice so low and so raspy that Phatty couldn't tell if it was a girl or a boy. "We are about the same size, slugger, so who are you kidding?"

Phatty, embarrassed by the comment, smoothed down his fur with his paws to make himself look as slim as possible.

"Raquel," said the raccoon finally, "but you can call me Rackie."

Phatty wondered if he could ever look at a banana again, let alone eat another one after this show.

Rackie stretched out her banana-slimed hand to shake.

Phatty, nervous to touch such filth, leaned in, smiled, and offered a paw-pump instead.

"So, what brings your hip-shaking, fur-flowing, butt-bopping self up on my rocks?" asked Rackie.

Rackie's comment "up on my rocks" was just the reality check Phatty needed, instantly reminding him of his predicament. He looked down the steep embankment of rocks, which he was still winded from climbing, and even though he was all the way at the top, he realized he had no way to leave his friends a message. He was mad at himself for climbing up before he had a plan.

Up. What comes up must go down.

It was at that moment that Phatty realized he hadn't planned on how he was going to climb down from here. His heart sank; this was too much to handle. He had no way to leave a note, he was exhausted, he had no plan, and it would be dark in a few hours. The reality of his situation dawned on him as he felt tears welling up in his eyes.

Coming to the park alone had been a colossal mistake, thought Phatty, and an even bigger mistake was thinking he could accomplish anything. Time was ticking away, and he had made no progress. He felt like quitting and just finding a way to run home, but as he gazed up at his home, it felt so far away and downright impossible to reach.

"Hello?" Rackie said. "You've gone all stiff, like you're gonna have a meltdown of gargantuan proportions. Hey, take a deep breath, will ya? It can't be all that bad!"

"It actually can," said Phatty. "It's a long story, and I'd hate to burden you with my troubles." Phatty sighed as he flopped down on the sun-warmed rocks.

"I got nothing but time," Rackie said. "Hit me with it."

"I should just give up now and try to find a way to head home." Phatty looked up, and he could see the railing of his beloved terrace. "There is no way I can do what I planned to do anyway. In fact, my 'plan' isn't even well planned out, and who am I kidding? I could never save anyone."

"Let me hear this story," Rackie said. "And allow me to judge the severity of your situation."

Phatty took a deep breath and started to tell the long tale

of him and the birds. He was about five minutes into the story when Rackie interrupted.

"Okay, I said I had time, but this here sounds like a really long story, so why don't you give me the abbreviated version—you know, the '*Cliffs*Notes' version." The raccoon chuckled, clearly amused at her cliff joke.

"Okay, short version. Hmm?" Phatty thought hard about how to put it into one sentence. "Big nasty hawk trying to kill me and my friends, steal my mom's jewels, and I left home"—he paused and pointed up to his terrace—"to come to the park to get to the zoo to tell the zookeeper how to get the hawk back, and I forgot to make a plan, and I am so stupid for probably worrying my friends to death and failing this mission, not to mention I might starve to death before accomplishing anything I set out to do! I have to just give up and try to get home." Phatty took a deep breath when he finished that sentence and rolled back over on the warm rocks.

"Puh, and may I add, *lease*!" Rackie exclaimed. "Boy, you talking downright trash, and I know all about trash, because trash is my thing, and to hear you saying you're going to give up after I just watched your pudgy butt climb those rocks—like a champ, I might add—and then you doing that dance, that rump-shaking, booty-quaking victory dance of yours, and now you're talking 'oh poor me, let me give up'? Oh, and news flash, you are far from starving to death, I can promise you that! Boy, life is about finishing what we start—persisting on a course of action in spite of any obstacles. Like bowling. You know bowling, right? When someone throws a large grapefruit at ten canisters of milk. They just blast those canisters of milk right out of their way." Rackie paused and waited to see if Phatty nodded.

Since Payaso loved bowling, Phatty knew bowling pretty well, but from the sounds of it, he wasn't sure if Rackie really understood bowling; Phatty couldn't remember any mention of grapefruits and milk. He didn't want to argue with Rackie, though, and since he got her point, he nodded for her to continue.

Rackie took a deep breath as she pretended to kneel and roll a ball down an alley. "Life is about learning how to push aside any of the 'trash' that gets in our way!" Rackie finished her speech with a deep and guttural banana belch. "Oh boy, I love those bananas, but let me tell you something, they sure as the heavens above don't love me! I will be having that banana over and over again for the next eight hours." She belched again, to Phatty's dismay. "Delicious. Well worth it."

Phatty thought about it. He still felt tears stinging his eyes; he was tired; and he felt sick to his stomach. Phatty couldn't quite put a finger on why, but he wondered if this was the feeling of being homesick.

He looked up at Rackie, whose humanlike hands were now parting each of her toes and picking at something Phatty could only guess was park "residue." He gagged at the sight. He sat up, her actions only making him more nauseated.

"I guess I have to deal with the hawk first? Right?" Phatty asked as he looked away from the raccoon's feet and hands.

"Greedy little buggers. Those things are flying, trash-stealing, poop-bombing pains in the buttocks," Rackie interrupted him.

"Yes, I guess. I mean, he never stole my trash or pooped on me, but he told me yesterday he was going to hurt my friends and steal from my parents sometime before today ends! I panicked. And now here I am, with only hours left to spare, and all I have managed to do is scare the dry cleaner half to death and get lost in one of the country's busiest parks. I can clearly see now that I am in way over my head. I let the birds' picking on me push me to act rashly. Now here I am, a hopeless cat, lost in the big city."

"Busiest parks in the country? Really?" Rackie asked.

Phatty stared back. "Really? That's your question? I share my heart-wrenching and scary predicament with you, and that's your only question?" Phatty asked, his voice a bit sharper than normal.

Rackie chuckled. "Don't mind me. I find facts about my home just fascinating. As for your predicament, I am able to see things a bit different from you." Rackie stood up now, stretching her legs for a quick second, and as if hiding from the sun, she instantly hunkered back down. "The way I see it is, standing before me is a cat so brave that he was willing to risk it all to protect his friends and family, a cat who at this very moment is a bit overwhelmed at his situation. But what I am sure of is, once this cool cat is able to see the forest through the trees, pun intended, he is going to realize that this situation is not all that bad. Tell me, why did you come to the rocks?"

"I thought if I came all the way up here, I could leave my brothers a message on the rocks so they could see from our home that I was okay. I didn't want them to worry, ya know?"

"Mmm mmm mmm," Rackie said, shaking her head. "See that, sugar? Even in the face of a catastrophe, you are still thinking about others. Boy, you are one cool cat!" Rackie's voice held real pride for her new friend.

Phatty paused, unsure if the raccoon was done talking. When she said nothing else, he continued telling Rackie the rest of his plan while playing with the strands of weeds in between the rocks with his paws.

Standing now, he finished with the worst part of his story. "But now I've realized I don't have anything to use to leave the message. Pretty silly of me, huh? I had planned to find the zookeeper at the Central Park Zoo to tell him that I found his missing hawk. It seemed so simple—*poof,* like magic, the problem would be solved. I would be able to prove to everyone I am not a scaredy-cat, return the hawk, and somehow save the day. But I don't even know how to find the zoo, let alone communicate with the zookeeper!" Phatty's voice was hoarse from desperation and thirst.

Phatty chuckled, reflecting, "And somehow, here I thought

I would make it home in time for dinner like some kind of superhero! Oh, and of course, let's not forget that I am being hunted by a crazy, mangled, very angry hawk who wouldn't hesitate to eat me, given any chance. Crazy stupid of me, huh?"

"Nah," Rackie answered, without any hesitation. "In my eyes, you're not stupid. Perhaps naïve, a little lacking in the self-esteem department, and just for pure honesty's sake, a tad shy in the planning department. I am guessing this 'mangled' hawk you speak of is the one with the messed-up schnoz and shattered talon, known on the park paths as 'Crawler'?" Rackie asked.

Phatty nodded glumly.

"Ahhh, shucks," Rackie said. "That bird is harmless, and let me tell you, he's all talk. Word around the park is he ended up in that zoo after a clown car hit him during a circus act. A circus act? I mean, come on. Who trusts clowns in this day and age? Pah-lease! They paint the smiles on their faces? Anyone with that much happiness to prove has got issues, if you ask me. And that obnoxious red nose? Don't even get me started on their shoes ..." Rackie shook her head. Phatty gave her a blank stare, and she corrected her course.

"Yes, Crawler," Rackie continued. "Well, this is what I heard. Once he got placed in the zoo after his accident, all of the other birds picked on him for his looks and strange circus talents. Word is they were so awful to him that they used to poop on him and try to hurt him physically and emotionally every day—that is, until he broke out. Hasn't been seen there since. But I'm not playing when I say that bird is talented—he was well trained, ya know, for circus acts. He can do just about anything! Shame he has a schnoz and a talon that could haunt a house. Heard his face and foot are so mangled that he is just about as ugly as they come. And you know how the birds can be. Those chirping little devils are not as sweet as the rest of the world thinks! Crawler has now been spending a bit of time on the dark side. Partnered up with a thief."

Rackie wiped her paws together and added, "Hey, but don't worry. I think I can help you out."

In one swift motion, the raccoon disappeared between some rocks. Phatty could hear her sifting through what sounded like piles and piles of garbage. "Not a shoe, no, not that one either, not a poop bag, not reading glasses, no, not a soccer ball, not a sweater, not used gum, oooh look, candy!" Wrappers crinkled, followed by a sucking sound. "Oh, wait—here it is!" And then, as quickly as she had disappeared, Rackie popped her head back up into view.

Phatty could see something white and thin in her tiny, humanlike hand. She reached out and gave the white, skinny object to Phatty.

"What is this?" Phatty asked as he reached out. The raccoon's claws were sharp, and Phatty was a little nervous to touch them.

"To be honest, I am not 100 percent sure," Rackie answered. "But I like to call it my 'magic stick.' I have seen kids use them over the years, and they always leave some behind. You can write on the rocks, and then when it rains, it disappears. I have quite a collection of them. And in colors!" Rackie said proudly.

Phatty got excited. "This is amazing!" he said, holding this "magic stick." He looked up at Rackie to thank her, but she was busy picking her teeth with her filthy feet. Phatty wouldn't have thought the raccoon's hygiene could get any worse.

"Try it," Rackie said with excitement.

Phatty held the magic stick tightly with his paw as if he were holding a pencil like a human would and drew a long line on the rock. "This is so great!" Phatty said with excitement. "I don't know how to thank you!"

Rackie was beaming, clearly excited her collection had helped her new friend. Luckily, much of the banana wedged in her teeth was gone now. Phatty couldn't help but imagine her cave full of garbage and other items she considered her "collectibles."

"Keep it, it's yours!" Rackie said. "I have plenty. And you can thank me by sticking to your plan and finishing what you started! Now you can leave your friends messages along the way, and you have a way to write the zookeeper a message when you get to the zoo!"

"Messages along the way?" Phatty asked. "But how will they see them?"

"Well, I could be wrong, but if you're not back soon, your friends and family might come looking for you. And if they do, you can leave them clues to help track you down. Don't discount the fact that your friends want to help you too, Phatty. You're one impressive cat, and my bet is anyone who meets you will want to help you."

"Thank you," Phatty said, blushing. "That idea is brilliant! Now I just have to think about what to write so Crawler won't understand."

"You could do symbols," Rackie said, and instantly Phatty had his plan. He would talk in code to Payaso like they always did when they didn't want his brothers to understand them.

"Where are you heading next?" Rackie asked, interrupting Phatty's thoughts.

"I am trying to get to the zoo," Phatty said.

"Hey," said Rackie, "would a map of the zoo help you?"

Phatty looked up, shocked, and asked, "You have a map of the zoo?"

"Of course! I have about ten of them," Rackie said proudly. "And hey, now that we're friends, maybe at night I will leave you messages from the rocks and you can signal down to me from your apartment."

"I would love that," Phatty said, beaming. Rackie had hunkered back down into her rubbish retreat to find a map of the zoo for Phatty.

"Hey, Phatty," Rackie said as she handed him the map. "Be sure to do something else for me, okay?"

"Sure, anything," Phatty answered.

"Promise you'll signal to me when you make it home safe? I'll be worried about you. And please, have a little more faith in yourself. Don't be so quick to call yourself 'stupid.' Be home before it gets dark, okay? Part of being 'smart' is not putting ourselves in dangerous situations." Rackie handed Phatty an old takeout bag from someone's lunch. "Use this to carry your magic stick and map."

"Okay, I will." Phatty's huge smile and newfound confidence were all the thanks Rackie needed.

Before long, Phatty sketched out a message to his best friend and to his brothers, packed his to-go bag, said goodbye to his new friend, and carefully navigated his way back down the rocks. Luckily, going down was much easier than going up. Once on the ground, winded from the climb down, Phatty headed toward a sunny place in the grass for a quick rest on something soft.

CHAPTER 13

While sitting in the grass, Phatty took a look around Central Park. It was so much more beautiful than he had ever imagined. Not only were there dogs being walked with their humans, but Phatty actually saw a pair of horses and riders trotting toward the bridle path that led farther into the woods. It wasn't scary; it was peaceful, with all the kids playing and having fun. Now if only one of those kids would share some food!

At that moment, Phatty was no longer a scared cat; he felt confident that his expedition was going to be a success. Thinking back to his new friend, he smiled and even chuckled as he pictured Rackie cleaning her teeth with her feet. Oh, the stories he would have to tell Payaso and his brothers! They would never believe what he had already seen—and already accomplished. After a few deep breaths, Phatty was ready to continue walking farther into the park.

Phatty walked around the baseball field, passed the carousel, and took a left at the Mall, the park's widest walkway. It was surrounded by a canopy of the tallest elm trees in America. As Phatty walked past the century-old sculptures of poets like William Shakespeare flanking the walkway, he was reminded of the beautiful poetry Payaso had read to him over the years. He cherished every moment, inspired by the poets.

Before long, Phatty saw a sign for the zoo. He was heading in the right direction! He laughed as he imagined all of the mismatched friends who lived together at the zoo. It seemed like at the zoo, you could be different and still fit in. How could a place like that be bad?

Excited that he was getting close to the zoo, Phatty reminded himself to leave a message for his friends. Getting out his magic stick, he found a clean large rock that was next to his favorite poet, and he began to write his friends a message filled with a poem and a sketch that they couldn't miss. He giggled as he drew, wondering if Payaso would even understand it—and more importantly, would they even look for it? *Well, I will later if I need it.* Like Rackie had said, he could use his drawings to find his own way home.

Phatty finished his message, and he continued down the path for what felt like forever to his short legs. The more he walked, the more tired he became. He was in need of a five-minute rest when he saw a beautiful pond only a few yards ahead of him. He paused and took in the serene setting, amazed by the beauty. Tall grasses waved in the breeze near the water. Lilies floated on the water. He was in awe as he watched all the people in rowboats soaking up the sun, enjoying their time in nature. He was surrounded by couples having picnics in the grass.

Phatty needed to take a break. Just a few minutes of rest would help the dull ache he felt all over. He walked to the edge of the pond to see if he could spot some fish while he rested his legs. As he looked into the water, he was startled at the cat staring back at him. He jumped back. When he looked again, he realized he was looking at his own reflection. Phatty thought that he looked very big and strong perched over the pond. *I certainly don't look like a scaredy-cat anymore.* As he was lost in thought, a turtle popped up, splitting his reflection.

"W-why d-don't you take a p-picture of yourself, k-kitty. That w-would last l-longer!" the turtle said.

Phatty was so startled that he lost his balance, almost falling right into the pond.

"Jeez! You scared me!" Phatty snapped at the turtle.

"W-whacha looking at, k-kitty?" asked the turtle. "Y-you've been s-staring into t-this p-pond for ten m-minutes, I h-had to c-come up and s-see what you w-were d-doing. F-from under the w-water it looked l-like you w-were going t-to c-come for a s-swim."

"Why do you talk like that?" Phatty asked the turtle.

"I d-don't know," the turtle responded as he turned to swim away.

"Hey, where are you going?" asked Phatty.

"Y-you're going to t-tease m-me now, r-right? J-just like everyone e-else?" stuttered the turtle.

"Tease you?" Phatty was hurt at the accusation. "Because you talk different? So what? Why would I ever tease you?"

"R-really?" asked the turtle.

"Sure!" Phatty exclaimed. "I'm Phatty!"

"N-no, you're b-big, but n-not that f-fat," the turtle responded.

"No, my name is P-H-A-T-T-Y."

"Ohhhhh," the turtle said, looking as embarrassed as a turtle could, and they both started to laugh. "Oops, w-well, my n-name is Greenie."

"Well, you really *are* green," Phatty joked. Greenie's shell was a dark, glossy green, and his skin was equally dark. They both laughed some more.

"What does your name mean?" Greenie asked.

"It stands for Pretty. Hot. And. Totally, Tabby. Yuppie," Phatty said proudly. "My guess is the *Y* was a tough one and they just tacked that on for fun." They both giggled.

Suddenly, Greenie stopped laughing. "Phatty, jump!" he yelled without stuttering.

Phatty was confused until he saw a hawk-shaped shadow moving fast over the water toward him. Crawler was coming! But diving into water was against all of Phatty's instincts as a cat.

"Phatty, now! J-jump in n-now!" Greenie called again.

Phatty closed his eyes, took a deep breath, and with every horror he could imagine running through his mind, blindly jumped into the algae-covered pond.

CHAPTER 14

"We have to move faster!" Stanley directed, nervously circling behind the cats. "Hey, look! I'm herding cats!"

Clyde kicked a pile of leaves at him.

Stanley slowed down and seemed to realize that Clyde and Payaso were struggling to keep up with him and Max; they were not used to so much walking. In fact, other than to go to the vet or sit on the terrace, Clyde had not been out of the house in eight years! And Payaso probably insisted on being carried around the world.

"You two are losing steam fast," Stanley said. Whistling to get their attention, he pointed to a new path.

They all followed Stanley without question. Payaso silently wished he hadn't spent his afternoon naptime horsing around. Clyde silently cursed himself for being so out of shape. They both came to realize that Phatty was not the only cat who needed to get in better shape.

No matter how tired they all were, the thought of Phatty all alone and scared kept them moving with determination. They took comfort in knowing they were all together. Until today,

Payaso and Clyde hadn't ever been friends. But as Payaso looked at Clyde trotting along desperate to find his brother, Payaso promised himself that after today, he'd be a little nicer to Clyde and include him in all the daily games.

"Hey, Max," Payaso called out. "What's your take on carrying a cat through the park?"

Max kept walking as he responded, "I have flaming red hair, loads of freckles, knobby knees, no friends, and rock constantly. I'm already a bull's-eye to the bullies at school. So what do *you* think my 'take' is on being seen by other students carrying a large cat through Central Park?"

"I don't know?" Payaso asked, unable to see Max's point.

Clyde and Payaso smiled at Max's funny answer. No boy, at any age, with any color hair and skin, would want to be caught carrying a fluffy, furry creature like Payaso through the park on a sunny afternoon. Clyde admired Max and could tell he was a good, smart kid, desperate to fit in. He was glad Max said no, because in his mind, Payaso needed to walk on his own in order to prove he was strong and independent enough for this adventure.

A few minutes later, Payaso, now even more winded and struggling to keep up, chimed up again. "Uh, Max, just clarifying …" Payaso tried to catch his breath. "So … was that a 'no' on the carrying a cat question?"

"What's the matter, Payaso, not used to *walking* the park?" Clyde asked, joking about the cat's earlier stroller confession.

"I would give *anything* to be in a stroller right now!" Payaso screamed. He was completely unashamed by his confession. At least Clyde had to give him credit for that.

Everyone laughed at Payaso as they continued on.

"Maybe I'm not used to walking in it, but I do love Central Park," Payaso said, pointing at different areas. "It's beautiful, and every area of the park tells a different story. Do you know that cottage was built in Sweden in the 1800s? It was used by the army in World War II! And back then, if they would walk through the park, people would be dressed to the nines in bowler hats, long dresses, and three-piece suits."

Clyde glanced around, clearly starting to enjoy Payaso's tutorials. There was so much activity, yet the setting was so serene and steeped in history.

Payaso continued, "It's almost like the park has its own heartbeat—the plants, animals, kids, you name it, it just feels alive. This is the kind of place I wouldn't mind getting lost in."

"Lost!" Clyde said. "After all this time, Phatty is still lost and in danger!" He continued searching garbage cans and calling out Phatty's name.

As Payaso looked around, he wondered what Phatty's experience in the park must be like. *Is Phatty enjoying the park? Does he see the beauty in the flowers and trees? How does he feel about being so close to so many people?* Knowing his friend so well, he thought, *He's most likely scared to death, hunkered down under a bush, too terrified to move.* His gut ached for his chubby friend, so kind and yet so meek and mild.

"Where in the world would he hide?" Clyde asked, stopping on the path for a moment. "Let's put ourselves in my brother's shoes, er, paws."

They all sat down for a moment, the cats breathing hard. Payaso's face scrunched up as he thought carefully.

"The rocks!" Payaso suddenly called out.

Max and Stanley raced toward the spot. When they got to the rocks, Max picked Stanley up and immediately started to climb. Clyde and Payaso were rejuvenated with energy; this was their first big break. Clyde made a few well-timed leaps and was at the top first, with Payaso following shortly behind, panting like he was gasping for his last breaths.

"Who's the brushtail possum now, Payaso?" Clyde asked, unable to suppress his grin.

Max was still climbing with Stanley in his arms, being careful not to stumble.

Payaso could not answer—first, because he was too out of

breath, and second, because he had just discovered something he never in a million years would have expected. It was a note from Phatty, written on the rocks:

Boyys Luk heer.

"That's him for sure!" Stanley yelled.

"I think we need to revisit his spelling lessons," Payaso mused.

On the rock, there was another cryptic message.

No tyme to talkiess. I needy to walkies.
This is mi furst cluu Im leaving for yuu.
Im using the majic sticks. Remember the timez ticks.
Becauz I goody at ryhmy, better thenz I
climby im off too the nexts place.
Maybee one dace, therre will bee a statuue of mi face.
Thenz I be walkies to the place wherz
beasts live of all kindz of race.
my friend givey me a mapp, don't worriez I takey a cat naps.

Below the poem was a bunch of drawings—scribblings really, of odd shapes with arrows.

"What the heck is 'dace'?" Clyde asked. "And 'talkie' and 'walkie'? What is he trying to tell us?"

Payaso was deep in thought, pacing back and forth. "He made it all the way here! Can you guys believe it? Phatty made it all the way here to the rocks!"

"But where did he find the chalk?" Max asked.

"The what?" Stanley asked.

"Cha—" Max began.

Payaso interrupted him, excited that he knew what chalk was. "Chalk!" blurted Payaso. "It is what he used to write the messages."

"I didn't know cats could write," Max said, smiling and

rocking slowly as he looked over the rocks. "And his rhyme wasn't bad, but someone needs to tell him that 'dace' is not a word."

"*But* he needed it to rhyme 'face'!" Payaso called out as he figured out the message. "He is headed to the Poets Walk! I taught him about the Poets Walk, and he remembered!" Payaso beamed with pride. "Give me one second. I will explain all of it." He stared again at the cryptic poem.

"He is talking in the code we came up with. We refer to things only he and I would know, so the hawks or birds can't figure it out. *No time to talk, I need to walk.* This is the first clue—he is telling us there will be more clues and that we need to watch for them. *I am using chalk,* for whatever reason he thinks it is called a 'magic stick,' *remember the time I rhyme better than I climb.* He is saying he will not be climbing anymore. He is walking the paths now. He's talking about the poets on Poets Walk, that's the face reference. He has always wanted to see the statues, and it is on the way to the zoo on the map. The zoo is where the beasts of all races live ..."

Payaso looked at everyone. Their faces were blank. "Beasts of all races? Hello ... animals of all different kinds live there! He then goes on to say *don't worry, I have a map of the park,* how he got that I don't know, and that he will be sure to take a nap if he gets too tired." Payaso finished, grinning with pride.

Clyde spoke first. "Well, Payaso, it is nice to see that the silly, off-putting, and secretive language you and my brother made up finally came in handy and was put to a good use, rather than being used to exclude myself and Stan."

Payaso wasn't sure if this was a compliment or not. He had never thought of the secret language as being exclusive, but now that he did, he realized that all these years Clyde and Stanley must have felt really left out when he and Phatty giggled and laughed, talking about things they could never understand.

"He also drew a stick figure and a horse, and if I had to bet, that is a drawing of a fish and a boat," Stanley said, pulling Payaso out of his dark thoughts.

"That's the caro—" started Max.

"Carousel!" Payaso finished before Max could.

"Is Phatty going to ride the carousel? Or going for a boat ride? Fishing? He's got to be hungry by now," Stanley said, thinking out loud.

Max thought about it for a moment. "Looking at the map, he is heading across the park toward the … carousel, then the path by the pond, and then, look, he is heading toward the …"

"Zoo!" Payaso yelled out before Max could finish his thought. "Like I just said, the zoo is where he's heading! He was worried we wouldn't get the poem, so he also drew a sketch … well, if that is what we can call this … his impression of the zoo. All of different animals holding hands."

"That's where he is headed," Max said in agreement. Before Payaso could interrupt him again, Max blurted out, "He is going to the zoo to tell the zookeeper that he has found Crawler!"

"Yes!" they all agreed, finally feeling like they had a chance of finding Phatty.

"Maybe he is trying to get Crawler to follow him there? And how will Phatty find the zookeeper?" Payaso was pacing fast now; there were too many unanswered questions. Payaso was frantic, Max was rocking faster than ever, and Clyde and Stanley both sat stunned at their brother's plan.

The faint sound of clapping startled them all back to reality, and simultaneously, they all turned around. From inside a small rock cave, they saw two beady eyes peering back at them. It was a raccoon, smiling at them.

"I'm impressed!" a raspy voice said. "I never thought you would be up here on the rocks! He told me you would be looking from up there." The raccoon pointed to the terrace way up in the sky.

Nobody spoke for a moment, then Clyde took charge.

"Excuse me. Who are you, and how do you know this about my brother?"

"I'm Rackie, and I met Phatty this morning." Rackie sat in her cave eating an old, dirt-covered hot dog. Ketchup and mustard were all over her face, and the hot dog bun was stuck in her teeth.

Rackie pointed to Stanley. "You're obviously Stanley." Then she studied the cats. Pointing to Clyde, she said, "I can tell you're the brother; you're a tabby too. Thinner, that's for sure. Boy, he wasn't kidding about that part." She moved on, studying Max next. "He never mentioned a kid, though."

Payaso whispered loudly to the group, "Nobody make any sudden moves. Raccoons can be very aggressive and dangerous while eating. And clearly"—he did his best to whisper—"they have repulsive table manners! Which is ironic, given that God gave them humanlike hands and features."

"Ahh, yes, yes, yes! You must be the know-it-all Payaso," Rackie said, looking proud of herself. "He described all of you to a T."

"Phatty said I was a know-it-all?" Payaso asked.

"Nah, I made an educated guess on that one. He said you were a walking encyclopedia, which is code for a certain condition called diarrhea of the mouth." Rackie winked as she laughed, then opened her large mouth and took another greedy bite of her trampled hot dog.

"See that, Payaso?" Clyde said with slow, meaningful sarcasm. "All you needed to do was run that know-it-all trap of yours for one second and a total stranger knew you must be the big mouth my brother adores!"

The group giggled. Rackie flashed another hot dog–filled smile, and at that sight, the group swore off hot dogs forever.

"Well, let's all be polite, thank the kind raccoon, and be on our way," Max began—and then immediately stopped when he realized something. "Wait a minute. If you spoke to Phatty, what else did he tell you?"

"Of course I spoke to him! That chubby cutie fetched me a banana. I was relieved when he didn't fall over from a heart attack after he finally made it up here. Determined fellow, that's for dang sure. And then, when he did make it up the rocks, he did that special dance of his about cake to celebrate …"

The group smiled at the thought of Phatty dancing.

"The 'Gimme a Cake' song?" Clyde laughed, remembering the hip-shaking, catchy tune that Phatty made up.

"Isn't that just the Kit Kat song with different lyrics?" Payaso asked with a smirk. Only Phatty could take a song about chocolate and turn it into a song about cake.

"Yep! But he insists it's his own song, so we just let him have it," Stanley explained.

"Well, it made me smile," Rackie said. "And then I gave him the magic stick so he could let his friends know he was okay."

"Magic stick?" Max asked, sounding amazed that the raccoon too thought chalk was magic.

"Duh, chalk," Payaso mumbled. "My guess is that this …"

Rackie let out a large belch before Payaso could finish. Payaso rolled his eyes and looked back at the raccoon.

"… this *creature*, I'm sorry, I mean *raccoon*," Payaso corrected, "was kind enough to lend it to him."

"So he told you where he was going?" Max asked.

"Of course he did!" Rackie said, now cleaning her teeth with her hands. Payaso wished he had a spare toothbrush to gift her.

"Why didn't you tell us before we wasted all this time figuring out his clues?" Max asked, his frustration obvious.

"I don't know—seemed like a big waste of the cutie's time if you boys didn't at least try. Poor little guy, took him three tries to draw everything. The first two times his own belly wiped away the drawings and the poem." Rackie smiled again, her teeth almost clean now. "But that didn't stop him! He wanted his friends to know he was okay, and he is desperate to stop the hawk from hurting any of you or stealing your family's stuff. I get that. I mean, I have some treasures in this cave that could stop a—"

"You know the hawk?" Max interrupted Rackie.

"Yes. Crawler is quite a legend here in the park! Hard to miss, wouldn't you agree?" Rackie twisted her face and her hand to mimic Crawler's deformity. "Word is, he's a circus hawk. Never can trust a bird that hangs around clowns, if you ask me. Big crazy red hair, crazy white face—no offense, gingersnap," Rackie apologized to Max and continued, "and how about the painted-on tears and crazy eye makeup … that's the telltale sign of a lunatic, if you ask me …" Rackie trailed off, looking up.

"Says the only animal here wearing a permanent face mask," Payaso mumbled.

A shadow formed on the ground in front of them.

"Speak of the devil," Rackie said. "That hawk is heading this way, so if I were you, I would take cover in here with me."

They all looked up to see Crawler circling them. Clyde and Stanley scurried into Rackie's cave.

"Payaso, get in here!" Clyde screamed, flabbergasted by his own alarm that the hawk would hurt Payaso.

Payaso looked into the raccoon's cave. He had seen cleaner garbage cans. In fact, he had seen cleaner toilet bowls. The cave was filthy, between the trash on the floor and the unknown liquids on the walls. And the stench coming out of the hole was enough to knock him over. And then, of course, right there in the middle of his worst nightmare sat the filthy, hot dog–covered raccoon.

"In there with you?" Payaso was horrified, wondering why no one had invented cat Purell.

"Payaso! Get in here!" Clyde yelled again.

Eyes wide, Payaso weighed the alternative. "I'd rather …"

Before he could finish, Clyde and Stanley pulled Payaso into the cave just as Crawler dive-bombed the group. The wind from the hawk's wings blew their fur back as all three of them toppled inside.

Max, obviously too big to fit in Crawler's talons, stayed outside the cave, ducking and doing his best to cover his face as the bird swooped by. With his feet, Max quickly rubbed away any sign of Phatty's message so Crawler wouldn't see it. The bird flew at Max again, and the gang in the cave screamed in horror as the large hawk released a stream of hot, bubbling, oozing poop that landed directly on Max's head.

Then, without wasting another second, Crawler flew off. Max stood motionless. The animals were still hunkered down in the cave, looking out in disbelief.

"Sweet creamy eggnog!" Payaso chuckled. "You got shiitake mushroomed!"

Max, now covered in hawk poop, said nothing. A full minute passed as Max silently absorbed the gravity of the situation. Poop dripped down his forehead, and he gamely checked his pockets. Rackie offered him a filthy napkin from her "collection."

"So, Max," Payaso said while Max tried to clean his face with his hands. "Since you're already covered in bird poop, what's your take on carrying a cat through the park now?" Payaso asked as he made his way out of the cave. "I could be wrong, but I'm guessing it doesn't seem so bad now, right?"

CHAPTER 15

Phatty surfaced from the pond, his whiskers slicked back, gasping for air and coughing up water as he doggy-paddled to the pond's edge. Greenie swam beside him with ease, coaching him the entire way.

"Y-ou're almost t-there, P-Phatty, k-keep paddling. D-did you s-see the s-size of that b-bird?" Greenie asked. "H-he was c-coming s-straight f-for you!"

"Thank you for warning me," Phatty said, reaching shore. He now had the real-world experience to prove that cats instinctively hate water!

Greenie guided Phatty to a hidden pond exit. His drenched paws sunk deep into the mud as he made his way up to the grass.

As he flopped over, catching his breath, he looked over at Greenie, and they both let out a loud laugh. Who would have ever imagined a cat and a turtle swimming together across a pond?! While Phatty cleaned himself up, Greenie confessed that his stutter was always made worse by nerves and fear.

"I'm sorry that you stutter," Phatty said, feeling bad for

him. “I know what it’s like to be picked on, and it’s a really awful feeling.”

“D-don’t be s-sorry for me,” Greenie said. “I d-don’t let them bother me too much. I j-just swim away or a-avoid th-them. I have p-plenty of things to be th-thankful for anyway. Who cares about a s-stutter?”

Phatty was taken aback by Greenie’s fearless attitude and said, “I wish I could be like that—you know, not letting anything bother me.” He explained to Greenie why Crawler was after him and all about the mean birds that taunted him on his terrace.

Greenie took a deep breath and looked at Phatty. “D-do you see my hard shell?” he asked, tapping on his own back with his foot. “I p-pretend this is a s-shield and n-nothing hurtful g-gets p-past it. I m-mean, sometimes it d-does, every n-now and th-then I hear s-something and I think, wow, that was h-hurtful, and s-sometimes I start to feel bad for myself—but then I th-think about how much I have that I need to be th-thankful for.”

“Like what?” Phatty asked, impressed with the turtle’s strength of mind. If only he had so much of that for himself!

“I can swim, I have a home, I can w-walk, and even t-though I s-stutter, I can t-talk! H-how m-many t-talking turtles d-do you know?” Greenie winked, knowing the answer: only one. “E-everyone needs a r-reminder to f-focus on what is g-great in our life, n-not what isn’t g-great. And we n-need to b-be t-thankful f-for it.”

Phatty thought about his wonderful family and fortunate life—his home, his parents, his brother, and his dear friends, new and old. He felt loved. He felt lucky. How many other cats had what he had? He knew, right then and there, he was never going to let the birds torment him off his own terrace again. And whenever he felt a twinge of fear, he’d remind himself not to feel scared, but rather, feel thankful.

“What are you going to do now?” Greenie asked.

As quickly as Phatty could, he told Greenie all about his plans to visit the zookeeper and get Crawler back to the zoo.

"Y-you better g-go," said Greenie.

"Hey, my mom loves turtles," Phatty explained. "She has turtle decorations all over the apartment. She would love to meet you, Greenie. Maybe one day I'll bring her here."

"That would be great!"

"Hey, you didn't stutter!" exclaimed Phatty.

Greenie smiled. "That's because you were so nice to me. Thanks, Phatty!"

"First, I'd better leave my friends a message. In case they come by, I want them to know I was here and that I am okay." Phatty reached into his small, now-bedraggled bag, pulled out the magic stick, and began writing.

Greenie watched and said, "I can give them a message if you want."

"That would be great," Phatty said. Phatty asked Greenie to tell his family and friend he loved them and where he was headed.

Greenie pointed Phatty in the direction of the zoo.

They said their goodbyes, and off Phatty went. *Another new friend!* he thought. *Just wait till I tell everybody!* Phatty felt himself walking with new confidence. He had used a magic stick, made new friends, left secret messages, swum in the pond, and even climbed rocks! He felt unstoppable! Now, aside from the creepy Crawler—who loomed above him somewhere in the trees, ready to pluck the whiskers right off Phatty's fine face—and the itsy-bitsy fact that Phatty might be lost, it was a great moment.

Phatty lost track of time as he walked on, and after a few minutes, he realized he'd totally lost track of the path as well.

He sniffed the air and realized that the pungent trail of animal aromas that had been leading him to the zoo had now vanished. He was lost. Panic began to set in. His heart raced again. Just as he was feeling full of anxiety, he heard a faint sound from behind the bushes. Phatty's ears perked up as he listened carefully to the little squeak. With his newfound courage, Phatty ambled up to the bushes to see what it was.

"Squeak, squeak, squeak," came the sound. As Phatty got closer, he realized the chirps were cries.

Phatty peeled through the bushes to find an injured bird lying on the ground, desperate for help. *"Sqqqqqquuuuuuuuueeeeeeeaaak!"* the creature cried, terrified.

The cardinal had a strange white spot on his chest, and it only took an instant for Phatty to realize this bird was one of the flock that always picked on him. Looking down now at the helpless bird—the bird who had terrorized him for years—he realized, for the first time, how enormous he was in comparison. *I've been scared of this little bird?* Phatty thought. He reached out to tap the bird.

"*Noooooooooooo*!" screamed the little bird. "Please don't do it! Please don't kill me! Please! Please!" The bird's wing lay oddly flat on the ground, and he seemed paralyzed.

Phatty was hurt by the accusation. "Kill you?" he exclaimed. "What the heck would I do that for? Clearly, I'm not an animal who kills to eat! My parents pour my kibble into a bowl and I eat like … well, I eat like …" Unable to finish the sentence, he got frustrated. "Well, I mean, just look at me. Aren't I the very definition of a posh house kitty?"

The bird's eyes went wide. Phatty looked down at himself. He'd forgotten about his swim in the mud and his long walk through dirt. He was a filthy mess.

"Well, I don't mean right now," he quipped, trying to brush off a few blades of grass adhering to his belly with chalk-covered mud. "I mean, normally, when I'm not on an adventure." That adventure had included mopping half of Central Park with his belly.

"You tell me," the bird snapped. "I opened my eyes and all I can see is this gigantic cat standing above me with a huge paw outstretched over my head! What else would you be doing?"

"Excuse me, I was just trying to see if you were awake! I was only going to poke you," explained Phatty, a hint of hurt still in his voice.

"Oh, well, I apologize," the bird said sarcastically, and she winced in pain while trying to move. "I have never met a cat who 'pokes' instead of kills."

"Well, thank you. I accept your apology," Phatty said, oblivious to the bird's sarcasm.

"Back it up! Will you please ... *back it up*!" the bird whispered loudly. "As you can now see, I am very much alive. Talking to a two-ton cat is bad for my image. In fact, if Crawler sees us talking, I'm a dead bird."

"Hey, I'm not two tons," Phatty cried out, his feelings hurt again. He adjusted his posture and pulled his belly in. "My mom says I am just big-boned, and for your information, I only weigh thirty pounds. My friend Payaso taught me that two tons would be four thousand pounds! I'm not even thirty pounds. And most of what I am is fur! And I am willing to bet that after the walk I just did today, I'm a pound down! And I skipped lunch too! So maybe now even two pounds? And whether or not you talk to me, Crawler is going to come for you. He's a hawk, and that's what they do. They prey on the weak, and small! Injured animals are the number one choice."

"Will you stop blabbering about your fatness and just go on your way and leave me be!?" the bird yelled.

Feeling like this was just another example of a bird hurting his feelings, Phatty started walking away ... until he heard the little creature crying again.

Keep going. This bird is the reason I am in this mess! He reminded himself of every reason to keep moving, but Phatty could not walk another step farther. Quickly, he turned around and returned to the bird.

"Don't cry," whispered Phatty. "I'll help you. If it makes

you feel better, I'm kind of lost too. I can stay with you. Or you can come with me."

"Just go away!" squeaked the bird, turning away from Phatty.

"I can't just leave you here. What will you do?" Phatty asked.

"I don't know." The bird began to cry louder.

Phatty stared at the bird for a moment, watching her cry, his heart breaking.

The bird sniffled, "And really, why would you want to help me anyway? I've never even been nice to you."

Phatty thought about it for a second, the years of abuse from the birds flashing through his memory. But as the bird lay there in pain, Phatty knew that the right thing to do was to help her.

"Well," Phatty began, "why don't we just start over? My name is Phatty." As a sign of peace, Phatty stretched his paw out again and gently tapped the bird.

The bird hesitated, shocked by Phatty's kindness. "Call me Birdie," whispered the bird. She winced in pain as she tried to shake Phatty's paw. "Thank you for not leaving me all alone."

Birdie then told Phatty how she fell out of a tree because she was scared by a squirrel. As Birdie continued, Phatty began to realize that they had more in common than he ever would have thought.

"You get scared too?" Phatty asked Birdie in amazement.

"Of course I do!" Birdie exclaimed. "All the time! In fact, sometimes my own shadow scares me! One time I thought another bird was following me in the park all day, so I kept running and running and it just kept following and following, and then when it got dark, it just disappeared, and I suddenly realized, that other bird was *me*!"

They both laughed and recounted stories about being afraid, and before long, Phatty and Birdie had become great friends. Birdie even admitted that sometimes she only picked on Phatty because she too was afraid of Crawler.

"Sometimes, with bullies," Birdie said apologetically, "you don't always do the right thing for everybody. Is it too late for me to say I'm sorry for all the mean things I have done to you?" Birdie asked.

"That's the funny thing about the word *sorry*," Phatty said. "I don't think it's ever too late to say it, as long as when you do say it, you really mean it."

"Well, I really do mean it. I'm sorry, Phatty, for everything."

Phatty smiled, and, from the bottom of his heart, said, "Thank you."

CHAPTER 16

Payaso and the others continued to search the park, following the trail Phatty had left for them. As they walked through Poets Walk, Payaso just couldn't help himself. "This is my mom's favorite part of the park," Payaso said. "Does anyone know why it's called Poets Walk?"

Nobody responded, and Payaso was so exhausted he didn't even feel like educating his friends. But as they walked by each statue, Payaso couldn't control himself, and he began to identify each literary figure's name: "William Shakespeare … Sir Walter Scott … Robert Burns … Wait, Robert Burns," Payaso repeated. "That was Phatty's favorite poet."

Just then, Max yelled, "*Look* down! Here is *a message*! Phatty left us a message!"

Buoys,
Momz favoriz thingys liv heer,
Lovy,
The phatty

They all stood in confusion, staring at the words below the statue of Robert Burns.

"He can remember a world-famous, insanely intense poet like Robert Burns, but he can't remember how to spell 'boys'?" Stanley laughed, dumbfounded.

"We are coming up to the pond," Max announced.

"Mom's favorite things?" Clyde said out loud. "It has to be turtles. She loves turtles, but why is he talking about a turtle?"

"Look over here," Payaso yelled, and he strode over to the water.

Tourists and locals sat at the edge of the pond sunbathing while others paddled around in small rowboats. The unmistakable and tempting smell of fresh popcorn drifted toward them. Off in the distance, they heard a saxophone playing. But there was no sign of Phatty.

"Keep looking for clues," Max called out.

Clyde ran around looking for anything turtle-related, clearly impressed by the bravery and intelligence of his brother.

As the four of them stood together at the edge of the pond, taking in their surroundings and wondering where Phatty was, a ripple in the pond caught Payaso's attention. He leaned down to see what it was. Clyde looked over and laughed at the sight of Payaso's long bobtail sticking straight in the air as his entire body perilously hung over the pond ledge.

"Everybody, come quick!" Payaso called out.

Clyde jumped over Stanley and dashed to Payaso's side.

"What is it? Is it Phatty?" Clyde yelled, his heart panicked.

"Look at the water. It's like a mirror! I can see my reflection—and look, now yours!" Payaso started making faces in the water and laughed at how silly they looked when the water started to ripple from the wind.

"That's what you called me over here for? I thought you had found Phatty!" Clyde growled with disappointment. He walked away to search the bushes, perhaps imagining Payaso falling face-first into the pond.

In the bushes, Clyde spotted something. How could he have missed it!? It was written right there on the ground, right in plain sight! A drawing of a turtle, and next to it, a message:

BUOYS, TAwkK TO MOMmS FAyyRIT

Just then, a turtle popped his head out of the water right in front of Payaso.

"A *turtle*! A turtle, come look! How cool, a turtle!" Payaso yelled with the excitement of a four-year-old. "Come look, guys! A big turtle just came up from under the water!"

"H-hello, P-payaso!" the turtle stuttered. "T-three cats c-came to v-visit me in one d-day!"

"Did you say *three* cats?" Clyde asked with excitement. "Phatty's note! It said talk to mom's favorite! He means you, doesn't he?" Clyde leaned forward and asked, "Mr. Turtle ...?"

"G-greenie. My n-name is Greenie," Greenie interrupted.

"Okay, Greenie, did you talk to the third cat?" Stanley asked as Max held him up to look into the pond too. Everyone was in awe of the talking turtle.

"Yes! His name was P-H-A-T-T-Y, a sh-shy guy, v-very scared, but v-very nice and v-very big-b-boned. T-that's the only cat I know p-personally, and w-we're f-friends!" Greenie said with pride. Then he continued on, without stuttering once, "That's one special cat! He was looking at himself, then he swam with me to escape the big bird, and then I sent him on the path to find the zoo."

Greenie detailed which direction Phatty was headed. It seemed that they were only behind him by thirty or so minutes. They were gaining on him!

"You just told me the best news all day!" Clyde said. "I can't thank you enough, Greenie, for helping my brother!" He jumped high in the air with joy. "Please, if there is anything I could ever do for you, don't hesitate to ask!"

For the first time in a long time, they sighed with relief, believing that Phatty just might be okay.

"C-could you h-help me with s-something now?" Greenie stuttered shyly.

"Anything," Clyde said. Even though Clyde didn't have time to spare, he knew helping Greenie was the right thing to do. Phatty would do the same.

Greenie pointed to a big rock on the side of the pond. "Do you see that rock over there?" he asked. "If t-that rock w-was in the w-water a l-little b-bit, I c-could c-climb up on it t-to b-bask in the s-sun but be able to j-jump b-back in the w-water quickly b-before another animal c-could g-get me."

"Sure, we'll help you," Clyde responded. He stared at Payaso. When the other cat didn't move, Clyde said, "Payaso, since this turtle was so kind to Phatty, I am sure you wouldn't mind helping Max and me move this rock and drop it in the water for Greenie so he has an island to sit in the sun on."

Payaso stared blankly at Clyde.

Clyde mimicked the motion of moving the rock with his paws at Payaso.

"Oh, we may have one small problem," Payaso whispered to Clyde. "I think in order for us to move that rock, we will need to go near that pond water, and I don't know about you, but I do not like water! Getting wet will ruin my fur!"

Without wasting a beat, Clyde shoved Payaso over to the rock. He looked right into Payaso's eyes and said, "We are helping this turtle, because not only does he need our help, but he was nice to my brother and your best friend!"

Embarrassed by his selfishness and fear, Payaso quickly responded, "Yes, yes, yes! Of course we will help him!" Payaso looked over at the water and then smiled sweetly at Max, hoping the boy would do the bulk of the work. "What's a little water on my pretty paws anyway?"

"I'll try to help," Max began nervously. His face was slowly turning the color of his hair. "But I guess now would be a good time to tell you that I don't know how to swim. If I fall in, well, let's just say that you would have a better chance at survival than me!"

Payaso was perplexed. "You can't swim? A young, healthy, and strong boy like you should be a fish in the water! Next week I will lend you a book of mine on the elements of swimming. We'll fix this fear of yours."

"That would be great," Max said. "Totally great."

Clyde pointed at the rock and hurried Payaso along. "Wait for my direction so we can do this quickly." Clyde explained his plan, and Max moved the rock to the pond's edge.

"Now all we have to do is place the rock in the pond," Clyde continued. "It's as simple as one, two, three … push!" Clyde directed. The rock was very heavy, but after Max pushed it all the way to the edge, they decided they would lift the rock together and drop it into the water.

"Hey," said Payaso. "I think all we need to do now is drop it in the water from the edge over here. We won't even have to get wet."

"Good idea," Clyde responded.

They lined the rock up at the very edge of the pond, ready to drop it in. Greenie paddled nearby in the water, obviously excited for his new resting pad.

"Okay, on three?" Clyde asked Payaso.

"Yes, on three," Payaso agreed, and they lined themselves up.

"One … two …" Clyde counted out loud. Just as he yelled, "three," Greenie began singing from the water—beautifully, with no stutter! He sounded so beautiful that Payaso was mesmerized. He stopped focusing on the task at hand and just stared over at Greenie.

"Watch your step, Payaso!" Clyde called out when he saw Payaso not paying attention and walking straight toward the edge of the pond.

"*Wooooooooahh*!" Payaso called out as he tripped. Still

holding the rock, Payaso lost his balance and tipped headfirst into the green, murky pond!

Greenie stopped.

Clyde froze.

Max and Stanley came to the edge of the pond.

Nobody said a word as they waited for Payaso to surface.

"Gassssp" was the first thing they heard as they watched Payaso reappear, flailing his arms and gasping dramatically for breath, his hair flattened to his face, his whiskers covered in pond scum, and his ears tucked straight back in an angry position. A tadpole jumped out of the water right onto Payaso's head.

"Well, the good news is, all of that dog saliva is off you," Stanley said trepidatiously. All five of them—even Payaso—burst out laughing, frightening the little tadpole, who quickly leaped off Payaso's head.

After all the stress of the day, it was such fun relief for Max, Stanley, Clyde, and Payaso to just take a moment to laugh. Clyde reached out a paw to help Payaso out of the pond. He now looked like a wet, dirty seal with his fur all slicked back to his sides. The laughter started all over again, with Greenie joining in. "You've made me feel so confident," said the turtle, "I hardly even stutter!"

From his perfect perch on Phatty's big terrace, Crawler laughed as he realized his master's plan was unfolding perfectly. All the animals had vacated the apartment just like he planned. Using his incredible vision, Crawler spotted Phatty and his new friend Birdie lounging in the grass. He felt a twinge of jealousy watching Birdie and Phatty, apparently instant friends, happily swapping stories, but he shrugged it off, knowing he needed to focus on his one and only friend, his master.

Watching the sun shift in the sky, he knew he had to focus on the time. He also figured, as it got darker, that the cat and bird might attempt to move, but that would be okay. They were easy to track, and he would take care of them after he got the jewels.

He began to sharpen his good talon, enjoying the sound it made as it rubbed roughly on the metal below him. It would be completely dark soon, and that's when he would make his move. He would have the jewels out and in his master's hands in no time.

CHAPTER 17

Birdie and Phatty were taking a five-minute rest under the shade of an elm tree. Phatty had been filling Birdie in on Crawler and the entire fiasco while they walked. Birdie had decided her wing was sprained; it was still much too painful for her to try flying just yet.

Now they were trying to figure out where the zoo was. They seemed to have gone off course, and they couldn't figure out what direction to go next. They needed to get moving while continuing to avoid Crawler. Tired and confused, Phatty was just about to tell Birdie he was ready to give up and go home when a nut fell from a tree branch and bopped Phatty square on the head! He jumped to his feet and looked up again, only to see a little squirrel looking down at him.

"Oops!" hollered the squirrel with a laugh. "I guess I should have yelled 'Whiskers up'!" The squirrel laughed again as he ran down the side of the tree to retrieve his nut.

"Hey!" said Phatty. "What do you think you're doing?"

"Relax, big kitty, I'm just grabbing my nut—unless, of course, you want it?" The squirrel put his hand out to offer

Phatty his nut. "Unless, of course, you plan to finally eat that little bird!"

"What?" Phatty gasped. "Eat the bird? Have you lost your mind?"

"Well, do what you want, big kitty," the squirrel said as he inspected his nut for damage. "But that bird won't last the night sitting here. In fact, if you ask me, she's a sitting-duck dead bird walking!" The squirrel burst out laughing at his own joke. Dropping his nut, he bent over laughing before dramatically falling onto his back. "Get it? I took the phrase 'dead man walking' ... and ... she's a bird, and I called her a duck!"

Nobody else laughed, and the squirrel stopped.

"I don't think it's funny to laugh at my friend who is badly hurt!" Phatty declared with a growl in his voice, glaring down at the squirrel, who jumped to his feet in fright.

"Jeez ... easy, big kitty. 'Tis life to laugh!" he bellowed out in a big booming voice before continuing. "Hey, look, take it easy! I was just playing! Don't get your fur all bunched up! Gosh, can't anyone take a joke around here?"

The squirrel quickly picked up his nut and began to scurry away. But before he ran back up his tree, he turned and cleared his throat. "You two should learn to look at life a bit lighter! Life isn't about getting to where we are going; it's about the adventure you experience on the way! Make this the best adventure of your lives. All you two are talking about is being lost and being eaten by Crawler! Blah blah blah. So what? He's a higgledy-piggledy bird with issues; well, news flash, we all have issues, *so move on*!" The squirrel was on a branch now, caught up in his speech. "How about I tell you the way to the zoo?"

"Perfect," Phatty answered.

"You missed the turn. When you get to the tall oak with names carved in the trunk, make a left. I'm Buttons, by the way. Would you believe that nuts have more calories than—"

"Uh-hum, Buttons? Where is the zoo exactly from there?" Phatty interrupted politely.

"Oh yes, so after the left, pass two garbage cans, a bench, and then you're so close … in fact, if you listen carefully, you can hear the monkeys and the birds. They are loud, and to be honest, very stinky. So when the smell is about to knock you over, make one last right. Then, voilà! You are there."

"Thank you," Phatty said politely, grateful for Buttons's kindness but careful to not spark any more conversation with the talkative creature.

"Hey," Buttons said, "don't miss the penguins and the sea lion exhibit. Those are my favorites. The bears are not so friendly, but they are pretty cool, but don't touch their food. Whoosh, I made that mistake one time, and let me tell you, it was not—"

"Thank you so much for all of your help, Buttons, but we should get going," Birdie interrupted. "Phatty wants to be home before dark."

"Hey, good luck to you both." Turning to Phatty, Buttons said, "You're the nicest kitty I've ever met! This is one lucky bird. Most kitties would have eaten an injured bird the second they saw it."

Phatty and the bird were about to leave when they looked back at Buttons, who was smiling, admiring his newest nut. They thanked him for his help and moved on.

The two walked together, following the route Buttons had carved out for them.

"It will be getting dark soon, Birdie. I'm wondering if I should take you home to my house first and then go on to the zoo alone. You're hurt, and you must be hungry!" Phatty said.

"Are you kidding?" Birdie asked. "I wouldn't let you do this alone, even if I had two broken wings and no feet!" Birdie smiled. They knew that being in the park in the dark alone would be trouble for both of them.

"Then let's get going. Once we get to the zoo, I'll leave a

note for the zookeeper, and maybe if we're lucky they can help fix your wing. Then I think we will go back to my house. You can recuperate there. I sure hope we will be home in time for dinner—I'm starving."

Birdie replied, "Now, I was just going to tell you to gently pick me up with your mouth and carry me, but then here you go yelling out you are starving, and that makes me a bit nervous!" Birdie looked up at him, only half joking.

"Oh, don't be silly," Phatty laughed. "I only eat kitty food! No birds in my diet!" With that, Phatty gently picked Birdie up in his mouth, and off they went.

"So if you don't eat birds, what do you eat?" asked Birdie. "I wonder if my cousin the chicken is on your menu."

"Oi eath ish an oi eath ain," said Phatty. With the body of his new friend filling his mouth, Phatty had trouble explaining that he only ate fish and grain.

Phatty's big teeth gently went up and down as he tried to talk without hurting his friend. "Whoa! Okay! Okay!" the bird cried out. "No more talking till I am out of your mouth!

"Ut ewe askd ee da westion!" Phatty mumbled, as he tried to point out that it was Birdie who'd asked him the question. Realizing how silly Phatty sounded trying to talk, they both laughed.

The light around them was fading as the sun began to set. They tried not to focus on the imminent darkness as they continued to walk in the direction Buttons had told them to follow.

"Imagine how silly we must look! A big cat and a little bird marching to the zoo," Birdie said to Phatty. Then, remembering she was in his mouth, Birdie said, "Never mind! Don't answer that!"

As the sun shifted, Clyde and Max went from walking briskly to running. The sign said the zoo entrance was around the corner; they were so close and felt the need to break into a jog. Payaso trailed behind with Stanley, who was also more tired than he wanted to admit.

"Wait!" Stanley yelled ahead. "You're going too fast! My legs are too short to keep up!"

Max and Clyde stopped running and looked back. "Max, why don't you run ahead and find Phatty. I'll wait for them. Let's plan to meet up just outside the zoo's entrance," Clyde directed. "You know what to look for, right? Phatty is a gray-and-black-striped tabby. He is quite large, almost thirty pounds, and from behind …" Clyde looked around to be sure nobody else could hear him. "Well, from behind, you would swear he is a raccoon. About the size of Rackie."

"Okay, I got it," Max said. "But since he doesn't know me, won't he run from me?"

"Just tell him this secret code: 'The pumpkins are ripe for picking on Tuesday.'" Clyde laughed as he said it, remembering when he and Phatty had made the silly code up. "He will be surprised at first, but just tell him you are friends with me."

Max's heart pounded in his ears, loving that word. *Friend.* It was official: he had finally made a friend. "Sounds great!" Max smiled as he ran ahead and then turned back in a panic. "Clyde, please be careful."

Clyde nodded, watching Max run ahead. Clyde smiled with a similar realization. The cat who disliked most people—heck, disliked mostly anyone—had just made a new friend too.

Max waved back and then headed toward the zoo entrance.

Clyde directed the others. "Let's start calling Phatty's name and searching the bushes as we make our way to the zoo entrance. We have to move quickly; it is starting to get dark."

Clyde, Payaso, and Stanley called out Phatty's name and checked every place they could—in garbage cans, under bushes, and even up trees along the path to the zoo. It was no use.

"What if we don't find him?" Payaso asked Clyde.

Exhausted and frustrated, Clyde began to feel sick. "We

have to find him! And once we do, maybe you will not try to talk my brother into doing crazy things anymore!"

Stanley yipped. "Hey, I don't like where this is headed. Clyde, Payaso said he was sorry."

"Phatty is lost because of Payaso's big mouth!" Clyde said. "Telling him to stand up to bullies! Look at what that did: *nothing* but get him into more trouble. Crawler could have him by now, and who knows if we will ever see him again."

Payaso twitched his whiskers nervously. "You know, Clyde, negative energy is the enemy. I read this whole book on these points in your body called *chakras*—"

Just then, Clyde toppled him, and they began to roll around in the dirt.

"I hate your books!" Clyde yelled.

They were so busy fighting, they almost didn't hear Stanley yell "*Crawler*!"

CHAPTER 18

With his new friend Birdie in his mouth, Phatty walked as carefully as he could. Something about the entire situation made him want to both laugh and cry: laugh because who could have guessed he would ever be in the park carrying a bird, of all things, in his mouth; and cry because he was afraid he wouldn't ever find his way back home. He tried to hide his despair and panic—especially because every time he exhaled, he knew Birdie felt a gust of wind. And cat breath!

Just as he was about to give up hope, Phatty found himself at the zoo entrance! He was overjoyed—but immediately, a hundred questions popped into his head at once. Which way to the zookeeper? How would he communicate with the zookeeper? Could he leave the zookeeper a note? Would the zookeeper even be able to understand Phatty's writing? Having not thought this far ahead, Phatty began to panic. He had come all this way to the zoo, but now he wondered, what if it had all been for nothing? If the zookeeper wasn't even there, what would he do? He needed a moment to catch his breath, calm himself down, and hatch a plan.

Phatty gently placed Birdie on the ground.

"What's going on? Why are we stopping?" Birdie asked.

Phatty flopped down on the ground, throwing up a wave of dust. "I need to take a break," he said.

"Excuse me? Hello?" Birdie tried to get Phatty's attention as Phatty began to shift the dirt around with his paw. "I get that you're tired and apparently fascinated with dirt, dust, and probably a huge mixture of old poop from a variety of animals," she snapped. "But we need to keep moving before it gets dark and the raccoons take over the park. Many of them are rabid, you know!"

"Old poop?" Phatty asked, horrified. "You think I'm lying in old poop?"

"Really?" Birdie asked. "That's what you got out of that statement? Lying in old poop is your concern? Nothing grabbed your attention about the darkness and rabid rats and raccoons? Of course it's old poop! This is a zoo! Look around us—animals left and right. They roam this place at night! As soon as the zoo closes, this whole place becomes the real zoo! Jeez! Don't you know anything? Cats!" Birdie let out an exasperated breath and sighed. "I'll just never understand your kind."

A moment went by as Phatty thought things over. He stood up and started to clean himself off, coughing with disgust as he choked on the dust clouds that formed around him.

Birdie watched Phatty. "Take your time, really. I guess you will want to be clean when the rats and rabid raccoons come for us," she chirped sarcastically.

Phatty stopped and looked at Birdie. "Hey, I have a friend who is a raccoon! We have nothing to worry about. And raccoons have the cutest little hands, don't they?"

"We are about to be lost in a dark zoo all night—or even worse, be eaten by something horrible!" Birdie exclaimed. "And all you can think about is how cute and sweet and nice the animals that could devour us are! What is wrong with you?"

"Technically, I don't believe raccoons eat anything that is

alive. Unless you consider a banana a living creature!" Phatty continued, laughing. "They scavenge for trash and leftovers."

Suddenly, they heard the shuffle of feet on the path, and then a tall shadow loomed over them. Phatty and Birdie froze. Out of the corner of Phatty's eye, he saw a skinny red-haired young boy standing behind them.

"Don't move, and don't make a sound," Birdie instructed Phatty. "I think this mini-human will walk away once he gets bored."

"Mini-human?" Max asked.

"OMG. He can hear us?" Phatty whispered.

"No, he can't," Birdie said.

"Yes, I actually can," Max said, blushing a color that almost matched his hair.

Phatty stood still. He was terrified of any humans he didn't know, fearing they would treat him like a big squeaky toy.

"You're Phatty, right?" the red-haired boy asked, and then he looked at Birdie. "But who are you?"

Birdie chirped her name and then looked at Phatty.

Phatty only meowed.

"I know you can talk," Max said, laughing at Phatty. "I just heard your whole conversation! We've been trying to find you!"

Phatty's eyes grew wide in shock. "Wait, you can speak with us, you've been following us, and you know my name? Are you an assassin? Sent here to kill me?"

Birdie stared at Phatty in annoyance over his silly questions.

"What?" Phatty said. "Haven't you ever seen *Mission: Impossible*? Or Bond? My mom and I watched the last one. Oh man, that first scene was crazy!"

"I know where you live!" Max said matter-of-factly.

Birdie now looked at the boy. Maybe Phatty was right.

Phatty stood frozen except for his eyes darting back and forth, searching for a place to hide.

"Phatty," Max said calmly, "the pumpkins are ripe for picking on Tuesday."

"I'm a dead bird walking," Birdie said.

But when Phatty heard Max's secret code, his ears perked up as all the fear washed away. He sat up straight and stared directly at Max, curious and excited now. "How did you know that?" Phatty asked.

"Clyde, Payaso, and Stanley sent me to come get you. To help you," Max said. "You can trust me. I am now friends with your brothers—and, of course, Payaso. He's a chatty one!" Max laughed.

Phatty was beaming with pride as he spoke. "Isn't he the best? He is so smart, and did he speak to you in any foreign languages yet? I've lost count of how many he speaks! And my brothers, they are so cool, right? I just adore them and—"

Birdie cleared her throat to gently remind Phatty that they were here on a mission they had to complete.

"We better go find the others," Max said as he leaned over to pick up the injured bird.

"No touching!" Birdie squealed to Max. "I'm sorry, kid, don't take it personally, but you touching me is bad for my image! You get it, don't ya, kid?"

"I sure do, better than anyone on this earth!" Max said, gesturing *I surrender.* "Then please follow me!"—he pointed in the direction they needed to go—"this way!"

"*Wait*!" Phatty yelled. "How did you meet Payaso and my brothers?"

Max smiled and then explained, "It's a very long story that we will have plenty of time to discuss later. But we've been looking for you together all day!"

"They're here? In the park?" Phatty stood up and stretched his sore and tired legs.

"Yes. They are waiting for us near the zoo entrance," Max said.

"But wait! I can't leave without finding the zookeeper!"

Phatty exclaimed. "I came all this way, and I need to make sure we get Crawler back into the zoo, or else I will feel like I failed everyone." Phatty sounded defeated.

"Before I found you, I found the zookeeper. He told me a lot about Crawler. I'll explain the rest later. But it's important we get home right now," Max said.

Home. Oh, after such a day, how great did that word sound? His green chair, his mom's meat loaf, his landscaped terrace—but most of all, his family and his friend Payaso were there. Home was his sanctuary.

"That sounds perfect," Phatty declared. "I should warn you now, Clyde doesn't have any fur friends," Phatty explained to Birdie before they began walking. "He might not be so, hmmm, how do I put it? 'Friendly,' yes, that is the word I'm looking for. Other animals, aside from me and of course my brother Stanley, are not Clyde's favorite, but he loves the human kind, and trust me when I tell you, the human kind love him."

"I should take some advice from Clyde," Max mumbled. "Apparently I do okay with the four-legged kind but I am not too popular with the Homo sapiens."

Phatty looked up, confused.

"Human kind," Birdie chirped, clarifying the word for Phatty.

Max continued as Phatty once again carefully picked up Birdie in his mouth and they walked on together. "I wish the human kind loved me—heck, I'd even settle for *liked* me the way you say they like Clyde. My mom says it's because I'm 'special' and that most kids don't 'get' special. I know it's hard on her when she sees me alone all the time. She gets so sad, and that makes me so sad. That's why I try to fit in, so she feels better." Max paused now as he kicked the dirt around at his feet and swallowed loudly. "Being this 'special' stinks, ya know? It's really lonely."

Phatty stopped too. "Well, it sounds like you have some new friends today, right? And, according to Payaso, animals are the better species. FYI, you should know that straight away to avoid *any* Payaso drama!" Phatty started laughing just thinking about his crazy, furry friend. "But you know him. He's biased."

Max's voice shot up a few notches: "I made some *great* friends today!" He was smiling now from ear to ear. "I love that you guys don't care about my orange hair, or my pasty complexion, or the freckles all over my face, or my knobby knees, or the fact that people think I'm 'special.'" He laughed now as he said, "I'm yellow mustard on a white T-shirt. I'm impossible to miss!"

"I like your hair," Phatty mumbled with the bird in his mouth. Dropping her, he continued, "It reminds me of sunsets and I think sunsets are pretty. And even though I just met you, you seem like a grand slam of perfection to me."

"Thank you." Max looked up and smiled as Phatty picked up Birdie and continued walking. He watched Phatty handling his onetime nemesis with such kindness and love. "I can see why your brothers and friend risked their lives for you. I'm Max, by the way."

As they marched along to be reunited with Stanley, Clyde, and Payaso, Phatty felt as happy as a kid on Christmas Day. Immediately, however, his emotions darkened when out of the corner of his eye he saw the big hawk soaring above in a large circle.

"Max! Look up! It's Crawler!" Phatty yelled. Without hesitation, Max moved as close as he could to Phatty and Birdie.

Then Max looked up at the big, nasty bird, shot his fist into the air, and yelled, "Crawler, if you want them, well then, you will have to get past me first!"

As if on command, the bird swooped down toward Max's face. Max threw up his hands to protect his face and opened his mouth to scream. And then they heard the recognizable sound of *splat tap tap* on the ground that had Max freezing in his spot.

Phatty and Birdie simultaneously screamed out the word "*Poooooop*," just as the all-too-familiar foaming, hot, liquidy material hit Max directly in his face.

Max closed his eyes and whispered, "Well played, Crawler. Well played."

There was no denying that Crawler had won this round too.

CHAPTER 19

Much to Payaso's dismay, he now found himself lodged at the bottom of an empty Central Park garbage can sitting on a half-eaten pretzel and covered in mushy, sticky, melted ice cream that had congealed in his fur. Yellow pretzel mustard covered half of Payaso's face, and the other half was covered by Stanley's backside. "You saved my life!" Payaso mumbled softly into the fur that squished into his face.

Stanley and Clyde were both piled on top of him. When Crawler dove out of the trees, Clyde had grabbed them, tossing them into the trash can for safety.

"Crawler was about to grab me, and you saved my life." Payaso paused, trying to shift the dog's butt away from his face. "I don't know what to say. 'Thank you' just doesn't seem like enough."

"You're tickling me!" Stanley yelled. "Your breath is blowing on my … fur and it tickles."

"Well, get your butt out of my face then!" Payaso urged.

Stanley, still laughing, now wiggled around, using Payaso's face as leverage to push himself over Clyde and poke his head out of the can. "No sign of Crawler," he reported. Then he barked, "There he is!"

Clyde quickly pulled Stanley back into the garbage can.

"What are you doing?" yelled Stanley with excitement. "Not Crawler! Phatty—and he's with Max! They're coming!"

Three heads popped out of the trash can, their jaws agape. Three pairs of eyes saw Phatty walking down the path looking calm, cool, and collected—with a bird hanging out of his mouth.

"Phatty!" Stanley yelled, his paw pushing off Payaso's head as he jumped out of the trash can and ran toward his brother. Clyde and Payaso followed, all screaming at Phatty with excitement. "Wonka doodle do!" yelled Clyde. "You ate a *bird*?"

"OMG! *No way*!" exclaimed Stanley.

"Impossible!" Payaso blurted out.

"Trust me," Clyde responded. "You guys don't share a food bowl with him. He does not handle missing meals well!"

Phatty found a soft place to put down the injured bird and greeted his brothers and best friend. "I'm so happy I could cry. I can't believe you've really come all this way for me." He gazed at them with appreciation and then stared closer. "Wow, you guys are a complete and total mess!"

Phatty giggled. He looked at Clyde, covered in dust from the paths; Payaso, stuck together with mud, twigs, and leaves, with streaks of vanilla ice cream and mustard; and Stan, whose fluffy white hair had turned brown with dirt and puddle water.

"Look at you!" Phatty giggled at Payaso. "You look like you rode a hot dog cart across the park to find me!" He laughed out loud.

Payaso touched his paw to his head and made a face as he felt the mustard and ice cream. All the animals laughed.

"*Clyde,*" Payaso growled, blaming him for the trash can.

"What? I saved your life, remember?" Clyde said, giggling even more at Payaso.

Phatty gently touched Birdie's head with his paw. Clyde's

and Payaso's attention immediately turned to Phatty's new avian friend. They prepared to pounce.

"*Nooooooo*!" exclaimed Phatty, shielding Birdie. "She's my friend! I need all of your help, and we have to take her home!"

Clyde took a closer look at Birdie. "I hate to break it to you, Phatty, but she looks as dead as a doorknob."

"Doornail,'" corrected Payaso as the group glared at him. "What?" he asked innocently. "The proper saying is 'dead as a doornail,' not knob. Fine, wallow in your own ignorance for all I care," Payaso huffed.

"*Really*?" Clyde grumbled. "You're going to go down the Mr. Know-It-All road right now, as my brother, a cat, has just admitted he is friends with a dead bird, and we are all in the middle of Central Park? Need I remind you that you look like a combination of a melted Mr. Softee ice cream cone and a pig in a sty?"

"But the bird still looks dead to me," Stanley said, crouching down as close as he could to Birdie.

"She's not dead," Max chimed in.

Phatty cleared his throat to get their attention. "Max is right. She's not dead."

"Dead? *Who's* dead?" chirped Birdie. She opened her eyes, came face-to-face with Stanley, and let out a huge scream. *"Don't eat me!"*

"Eat you?" Stanley asked. "Why would I eat you? I don't eat birds! Birds live in their own feces. Yuck! Besides, I only eat chicken."

"Technically," said Payaso, "a chicken is a—"

"Payaso, zip it!" everyone said in unison before he could start lecturing.

"I hate to break up the reunion," Max chimed in, "but we need to get back. I've figured out what Crawler has planned, and we need to get to the apartment right away."

They all stared at him. Up until now, they were too busy oohing and ahhing over finding Phatty to notice the large amount of fresh bird poop that clung to Max's clothing and hair.

"Well, you can't drop a bomb like that and leave us hanging. What's his plan?" Payaso blurted out, unwilling to be the first one to draw attention to the poop. It was, after all, the second time today that Max had been attacked by Crawler's backdoor firing squad.

"Speaking of dropping a bomb ..." Stanley giggled. "Do we even want to know?" he asked, indicating the mess.

Before Max could answer, Clyde chimed in as he walked around Max, checking the damage. "My goodness, what does that bird eat? I mean, come on! If you ask me, that's a record-breaking amount of Dunkin' Doonuts for one day."

"Let's just pretend I am not covered with poop, yet again." Max blushed and continued. "I will tell you more later, but here is what I think: Crawler does plan to steal your mom's jewelry. What was the one thing he had to do to perfectly execute his plan?"

Max was met with blank stares and silence from all of the animals.

"Get you guys out of the house!" he shouted.

"So this has been his plan all along!" Stanley said.

As they raced out of the zoo, Max quickly brought his friends up to speed. When he had found the zookeeper and told him all about Crawler, the zookeeper realized immediately what was going on.

Crawler's real name was Wally Otis. Ironically, the zookeeper loved Wally Otis. The circus rumors were true; Crawler had been trained to do tricks by a circus group, like open doors, fetch, and even perform a very funny version of the moonwalk. The zookeeper was devastated when Crawler went missing.

"He wants desperately for Crawler to be returned, especially since he missed the chance to tell Crawler how much he really cared about him," Max explained. "He felt bad for Crawler, always getting picked on by other birds and never finding any friends. The zookeeper wanted to show Crawler he could fit in if Crawler just gave the zoo one more chance." Max finished his story just as the group made it to the road in the park. Max waved down a pedicab.

"What are you doing?" Phatty asked Max.

"I am getting us a ride. I have some money on me, and this will get us home much faster than on foot," Max explained as the pedicab rode up to them. "Now, don't talk to me in front of the driver. I already look crazy rolling around the park in a pedicab with three filthy cats, a half-dead bird, and a small mud-covered dog!"

Max turned to the driver, who had stopped the pedicab in front of them, and showed him a piece of paper that had his address printed on it.

The pedicab driver said, "Hop in, kid. That address is a quick ride across the park." He just stared at the animals and then back to Max and the poop in his hair. "These animals all yours, kid?"

"Y-yes. W-we need to g-get home f-fast," Max answered softly as the man looked the filthy animals over.

The driver paused before responding. "Quite an odd collection. Seems that cat, the one missing his tail with the funny feet, got ahold of some mustard." The driver just stared at Payaso.

Payaso shot him a dirty look. "Is he talking to me? I haven't even had a hot dog," he hissed, still unaware that mustard covered most of his head.

"Next time, you should consider tossing those cats in a stroller!" muttered the driver as he shook his head.

"*See*?!" Payaso yelled. "Ah-ha! A stroller. Everyone made fun of me, but now who wishes we had a stroller? Because three cats, a bird, a dog, and a ginger-haired boy riding across Central Park in a pedicab looks totally normal! Now what do you think your friends will say?"

"You are my only friends," Max said softly as he looked at the animals with love.

We are his only friends. How is that even possible? He is so smart, so nice, and so fun! Pizzle sticks! Payaso couldn't imagine Max not being the most popular kid at school. *I mean, he talks to animals. Can it get any cooler than that?*

All Payaso could do was pat Max on the leg with his paw. He lovingly leaned into him as Max started to pick the mustard out of Payaso's fur. Max gave Payaso an affectionate squeeze.

"Well, speaking of friends, can anyone guess how many I made today?" Phatty asked.

"Friends?" Payaso asked. "You don't mean Rackie, do you?" Payaso shuddered as he pictured that wild animal's manners.

"Yes, of course! She was great. And Greenie the turtle, Buttons the squirrel, and of course, Birdie," he said, looking down at his new small and wounded friend.

"We met a bunch of them," Payaso explained.

"Weren't they great?!" Phatty exclaimed.

As the pedicab pedaled away toward the park exit, they all swapped stories of the adventures of the day, and Clyde laughed as he told Phatty about Payaso falling into the lake. Phatty loved the idea of his brother and his best friend working together. Phatty then went on and on about all of the new friends he had met along the way.

The ride along the park felt nice. They all sat back and enjoyed the scenery as the cab rode along so many of the trails they all had traveled earlier that day. Joggers, dog-walkers, and kids in strollers were all interspersed with the wildlife in the part.

"This is the way to see the park," Phatty said out loud. "I could get used to being rolled around!" They all laughed, still thinking of Payaso in the stroller. "Hey, did you get the notes I left you with the magic stick?" Phatty asked.

"You mean chalk." Payaso looked at Phatty. "Nothing magic about it. It's just a combination of magnesium silicate and calcium sulfate. Chalk is just soft rock that is formed under marine conditions."

"Yes, they were great clues, Phatty," Clyde said, before Stanley could bring up Phatty's horrible spelling. "We all thought they were perfect. Didn't we, Stanley?" Clyde shot Stanley a *zip it* look.

Phatty called out, "Hey, do you guys see that tree right there?" Phatty extended his paw. "I have great news: a squirrel named Buttons lives there, and he told us how to get back from here, this exact spot, just in case we ever get lost again!"

"Did he say a squirrel named Buttons?" Payaso asked. Phatty answered, but Payaso heard nothing. His mind was spinning over Phatty's new friends.

How will Phatty have time for me with all of these new people and animals? Birds, squirrels, a talking turtle? And Max, cool and awesome Max, and to make matters worse, this awesome, talking mini-human lives in the building. How can anyone compete? What will happen when I am gone? He won't even miss me. He won't have time *to miss me!* Payaso was now in a heartbroken panic.

The cab arrived at the corner of their apartment building. It had been under five minutes from Buttons's tree to the shed. While Max paid the driver, Clyde jumped out and fetched their disguises from the shed.

"You're a crazy pair of friends," Max laughed as he watched Clyde and Payaso don their disguise.

"Friends?" Clyde questioned. "Me and Payaso? We disagree on everything! And he has a baby carriage! I can't be friends with a cat in a baby carriage!"

"Well, you look like friends to me," Max said. "I mean, you two just spent the day in the park working together to find Phatty. That seems like friendship to me. Friends are meant to have different thoughts and opinions, and all friends argue. The baby carriage part … well, it is a bit odd, but who are we to judge?"

"Max, will you come up with us to help with Birdie?" Phatty asked.

"One hundred percent, friend," Max answered quietly.

"Well," Clyde said as he put on the raincoat, "now you have five different friends. That is, if you want to count Payaso and that big-mouthed bird. But don't say I didn't warn you! Payaso gets annoying fast!" Clyde pretended to push a baby stroller with his free paws.

They all laughed, even Payaso.

"I would be honored to help you. And you're right—that's what friends do for each other!" Max said.

"Yes, Max," Phatty said. "That's exactly what friends do!" Phatty smiled. "And Max," Phatty added, "*we* all think 'special' is *great*."

Quickly, they rushed to get dressed again like the dog-walker, only this time, they needed to make room for Phatty in the tower and Birdie in the coat pocket.

"Okay, guys, who is on top?" asked Phatty.

"*Not* you," they all said together.

Payaso eagerly went to reach for his hat but saw that Clyde had it on already. Ordinarily he would protest, as Payaso considered himself by far the best suited to be atop the cat tower, but given what they'd been through, he decided to let Clyde take the lead. With Clyde on top, Payaso was sandwiched in the middle.

"Think of it like this," Phatty said with a warm smile. "You are like the center of the Oreo—the glue that holds us together."

"Step on it, boys, we have to stop Crawler!" Max urged them. Payaso took a moment. Was that true? Was he the glue that held everyone together? His heart was once again filled with hope.

"I wish I could just carry you guys into the building," Max exclaimed as he snapped the raincoat's buttons together. "But the doorman will never understand how I went to the park and came home with three cats, a dog, and a bird I have never seen before. I'm pretty sure he'll call your parents or my parents, and then who knows what would happen. How could we explain how you got to the park in the first place?"

"You are right," Payaso said to Max. "You don't know us; it would be impossible to explain; and I would worry the building's management would think you tried to kidnap us or even worse!"

Max closed the last button on the jacket and stepped back. "Now this looks even better!" Max exclaimed as he gave the tower an up-and-down review. Payaso noticed that for the first time today, Max had stopped rocking. "Look, with Phatty in the tower, the coat is no longer dragging on the floor!" Max then attached Stanley's leash and handed it off to Clyde. Once the cats and dog were all in place, they steadied themselves as Stanley began his slow walk toward their building.

Max walked behind them, clearly anxious to see his new friends make it home safe and sound, and ready to grab the tower if it began to fall.

"Slow down, Stan. I can't move that fast on two legs," squealed Phatty.

"I've seen how fast you 'don't move' on four legs," laughed Stanley.

"Remember, walk through the lobby without making a sound!" Clyde instructed, and he cleared his throat and looked down, making sure Payaso knew the comment was meant for him.

They entered the building, walking past the front desk and giving a nod to the doorman. They picked up the pace so the doorman wouldn't have time for small talk, but the faster they walked, the more the tower stumbled and wobbled, drawing more unwanted attention.

Payaso saw the doorman about to make a comment. Just then, Max yelled out a loud cheerful "Hello," offering the doorman a high five over the front desk counter. The doorman greeted Max with good cheer and waved the cat tower on. The cats meandered toward the elevator bank just as the doors opened.

"Holy Mother of Madison!" Clyde shrieked as the dog they'd met earlier strolled off the elevator directly into them. "Not Moo again!"

Moo charged ahead on his leash toward them, jumping around viciously. His owner struggled with all his strength to control the dog, who was doggedly determined to make contact.

The cat tower froze. If they turned back, they had a big chance of the doorman catching them, but if they continued on, they'd be a cat snack for the dog.

The tower teetered backward and forward, and Phatty squealed nervously as he fought to hold up more than fifty pounds of feline above his head. Payaso thought for sure they were going over like a tree being chopped down. Just as all hope was lost, the man regained control of Moo and kept walking. The tower tumbled forward, crashing into the open elevator just as the doors began to shut. The cats fell out of the raincoat like oranges spilling out of a grocery bag. Head over feet, they rolled to a stop, making sure that Birdie was still safe and sound inside the coat pocket. Just as the doors closed together, Phatty wedged in his paw, holding it open for Max.

"Hurry up!" Stanley yelled. Max skidded by Moo and his owner and landed inside the elevator. Stanley hit the button for floor nineteen. As the doors closed, all three cats waved to Moo, who stood with his owner, both of their mouths open, as they appeared stunned by what they'd just seen.

"Did you see his face?" Payaso howled.

"Who could miss it?" laughed Clyde.

"The dog looked more shocked than the man!" Phatty chimed in.

"What's so funny?" asked Stanley, who sounded unamused. "How will I ever face that dog again? That dog is going to tell everyone that I get walked by three cats. I am ruined!"

Stanley's despair only made the cats laugh harder.

As they approached the nineteenth floor, Max and Clyde began to organize a plan. When they stepped off the elevator, Clyde said, "When we get into the apartment, Stan will hide Birdie under the couch. Then Max and I will figure out what to do with Crawler."

Payaso looked at Phatty, so bedraggled-looking, so filthy, yet with a confident glow about him that Payaso had never seen before. "And Phatty and I will help with the plan to deal with Crawler. Once and for all!"

CHAPTER 20

The elevator door opened, and the group barreled onto the nineteenth floor, out of breath and on a mission. As Max opened the front door, he yelled, "Be on the lookout for Crawler! He could be inside!"

Entering the apartment quietly, Phatty saw Crawler opening up the second window. They all froze with fear. The screen on the left window had already been torn, but the first booby trap had worked. The detached cords hung limp, leaving Crawler's feathers wedged in the window screen. Phatty glanced at the window on the right with bated breath. The second booby trap was ready to spring into action.

Crawler started working up the window, trying to peel back the Scotch tape holding the window closed.

"No, he can't get away!" Phatty cried. He leapt forward just as Crawler finally got the window open. Phatty snapped the Scotch tape. That pulled the strings taped to the confetti cannons, and *boom*.

The cannon shots of confetti jolted Crawler backward and flew like pixie dust into the wind, blinding the hawk. Crawler looked like a shocked, trapped bird inside of a shaken snow globe. As he tried to regain his footing, he stepped back, and *bingo,* his large talon triggered the net, which came flying down, landing right on his head.

"*Squaaaawk*!" Crawler shrieked as he panicked and fought in the net. "What the heck? Help me! Help me! Oh geez! Oh geez. Get me out of here!" Phatty followed the bird's panicked gaze as he looked over to the rocks for Norman's assistance. Then, for one brief moment, Crawler locked eyes on Norman; his binoculars were pinned on the terrace. Crawler felt a chill just as the man got up, turned his back on Crawler, and walked away.

Clearly, Crawler was now on his own. The feeling of being deserted by the man he thought was his only friend was almost as painful as being trapped in any net. Pain turned to rage, and Crawler struggled even harder to free himself. He screamed and flapped his wings, unknowingly entangling himself further.

To the cats' delight, Crawler wrapped himself up all on his own, his talons stuck inside the net's webbing. He was totally and completely trapped.

"It worked!" Max called out. "Both traps did exactly what you planned!"

They all stood shocked, staring in disbelief at the windows. Phatty felt a bit surprised that their shifty homemade traps had actually worked. They waited for the moment when Crawler finally accepted his own predicament, and soon enough, Crawler stopped fighting, let out a deep breath, and froze, shoulders slumped, staring at the ground, defeated and sad. Resigned, Crawler gazed at his captors, his eyes wide with fear and dismay.

Phatty was saddened as he read Crawler's expression. He knew what it felt like to feel trapped—even if the trap was only your own fears and worries. Phatty was no longer scared of the large bird, now safely ensnared. Thinking about the zookeeper's story and Crawler's injuries and past, Phatty realized what he most felt was sadness.

"Crawler, I ... uh ... mean *Wally,*" Phatty said softly. "Are you thirsty or hungry? We don't want you to be uncomfortable in there. Just give us some time to get you untangled, and Max here is going to help us get you home."

All of the other animals and Max turned to stare at Phatty, jaws open.

"Tufted titmouse!" Birdie yelled, emerging from her hiding spot.

"What?" Phatty asked. "A little kindness goes a long way."

"Phatty, within the last twenty-four hours, that bird almost ate us on ten separate occasions," Payaso said matter-of-factly.

Phatty continued, working up the courage. "Had this, Crawl ... I mean, haw ... I mean Wally, yes, if Wally here really wanted to, he would have eaten all of us the second we left this house. But he didn't. He only tried to scare us, because deep down, I think he knew better."

"Oh, Jumpin' Jehoshaphat," Clyde interjected. "He's a mean bird!"

"And a bully," Payaso reminded his friend.

"But I know how it feels to be different," Phatty answered calmly. "And from what I have heard, Wally has had a rough life. Up till now. And from here on out, I am going to show Wally only kindness." Phatty turned to all of them. "And I hope all of you join me. Because if I have learned anything, it is that we should all treat others how we wish to be treated ourselves. Because a little kindness goes a long way."

Wally listened raptly to Phatty's entire speech. Tears moistened his big black eyes. Embarrassed by his show of emotion, he struggled in the net to turn away from the witnesses to his tears. Max, without saying a word, walked over, carefully picked up the net, and started to untangle Wally's talons to make sure Wally was comfortable.

"Sorry about the poop thing," Wally mumbled through quiet sobs.

Max smiled and laughed. "Oh, please, what's a little poop among friends, right?"

Wally's eyes went wide; he appeared too stunned by Max's kindness to answer.

"What's our plan?" Clyde asked skeptically as he watched Max untangle the now subdued bird. Clyde never took his eyes off his new friend Max.

"The zookeeper misses Wally and has been worried sick about him," Max began.

"Ernie was actually worried about me?" Wally asked.

"Very much! He's been looking for you every day!" Max took out a flyer from his pocket that the zookeeper had given him. It said *LOST* with a picture of Wally and information and even a reward for his safe return. "He promised that he's going to make sure you have a much better life once he gets you back safe and sound. He told me how all the other birds treated you, Wally Otis, and I was sad to hear how hard of a time you had while living there. And I'm sorry about the accident at the circus."

"Please don't call me Wally Otis," Crawler squawked and then continued, "I am Crawler now; it is a much tougher name. No one teases a mean bird."

"Well, you're not a mean bird. You are a sweet and talented hawk named Wally who lives at the zoo," Phatty said. "And I happen to like the name Wally way more than Crawler. Why don't you try using that crazy Crawler personality for good now instead of evil?"

"I guess it can't hurt to try," Wally said. "'Waddling Wally,' that's what they called me at the zoo." Wally looked defeated.

Max laughed. "Well, 'Waddling Wally,' take if from someone who gets called Gingersnaps, Agent Orange, Annie, Pumpkin Head, and much, much more: who cares?! I like you, and from here on out, I'm going to come visit you at the zoo, and I will be your first friend."

Wally looked stunned. A real friend? "You are going to be my friend?" Wally asked as if he wanted to make sure he had heard correctly. "Even after I pooped on your head?"

"Yes," Max laughed, followed by the group. "Even after you pooped on my head."

"But … why?" Wally asked.

Phatty answered for Max. "Because everyone deserves a second chance, Wally. And because everyone deserves to have a friend."

With that, Max put Wally right on his shoulder, gently stroking the bird's chest feathers and briefly touching the twisted beak.

Wally was overcome with tears of joy. "I am not sure if I could ever express, in words or actions, the level of how sorry I am for not only being mean and treating you all bad but bullying you and for scaring you. I am very sorry, and I hope you give me the chance to make it up to all of you." He cleared his throat and continued emotionally, "And let me finish by saying thank you. Thank you for giving me another chance and for being kind to me even when I didn't deserve your compassion or your help."

Phatty clapped and yelled out, "Apology accepted, El Toro!"

Everyone clapped. Payaso stood frozen, speechless. He was dumbfounded as he watched Phatty go running over to Max so he could high-five the hawk.

"You're really going to come and visit me?" Wally asked Max.

"Yep, this very Monday!" Max answered.

"Wow! Oh, wait, don't come on Monday. Ernie gives me a bath on Mondays. Come Tuesday. I like Tuesdays. It's a day of the week that nobody ever pays attention to. Monday is dreaded, Wednesday is hump day, Thursday is 'almost the weekend' day, and well, you know the rest. But Tuesdays—Tuesdays are just boring, and I feel that anything boring needs to be celebrated." Wally's voice was different now. It wasn't the pretend voice of an evil bird he'd used before; it was now a kind, gentle, innocent voice. "Do you promise to come?" Wally asked.

"I promise," Max declared. "I know what it's like to need a friend, and I'm really excited to make a new one!"

"Okay, then, could you sneak in some apples for me?" Wally asked. "I love them. Also, can we work on a new nickname for me? Maybe something cooler than 'Waddling Wally'? I'm trying to get something hip to stick, like—"

"El Toro!" Phatty called out.

"Yes! I love that!" Wally exclaimed. "And maybe I can call you something cool? What do you think about a secret handshake?" Wally rose and stretched out his wings with excitement. "None of the other birds has a human friend. This is going to make me the coolest bird in the zoo!"

All of the animals laughed as they listened to Max and Wally make plans. Max called over to the zoo and set up a time and place for Ernie the zookeeper to pick up Wally and get him back to the zoo safe and sound. As everyone waved goodbye to Wally, the hawk said, "Until we meet again, my friends!" Wally waved one more time to the group as he and Max headed toward the elevator.

Max looked back, smiled, and said with certainty, "I'll see you guys tomorrow!"

Phatty, Payaso, Clyde, and Stanley cleaned up the terrace and traps as best they could, but exhaustion soon crept in.

"I'm ready to nap and *eat*!" Phatty said, and everyone laughed.

"Hey, Birdie is probably hungry too, Phatty. Make sure you give her some of your food," Payaso said.

"*My* food?" Phatty stopped in his tracks.

"What did you think the bird would eat?" Stanley asked.

Phatty had clearly not thought about sharing his most valued possession: food. Everyone started to giggle because of the worried expression on his face.

"Don't worry, she eats like a bird!" Payaso kidded.

As the group swapped jokes, Payaso pulled Phatty aside for a second. "First, I want to say how proud I am of you—not only for the way you forgave Birdie but also for the way you helped her and for the incredible way you were able to see something in Crawler when nobody else could. Your humility and ability to forgive and be kind when others most likely cannot astounds me. I am the one who learned from you today, and I am proud to have ever called you my friend."

Payaso stopped for a moment, quiet and reflective.

"I also want, actually need, to say that I'm sorry too," Payaso said softly. "Phatty, you could have gotten hurt today, and I shouldn't have pushed you to be more than you wanted to be. And I need to apologize to Clyde and Stanley. I put them at risk too."

"Don't be sorry, Payaso. I should be thanking you," Phatty said. "Thank you for having faith in me! Because of you, I made so many new friends today, and I even stopped a criminal and helped Wally get back home!" Phatty beamed, and then he began to describe each of his new and wonderful friends.

As Phatty told tale after tale, Payaso began to look very sad rather than joyful and celebratory. Phatty was beginning to worry that maybe his newfound courage and confidence might make Payaso feel like their special friendship had come to an end. He imagined that Payaso would feel lost if he thought his friend no longer needed or missed him. Payaso did have a big mouth, but he had an even bigger heart, and that's what Phatty had known all along.

The tears Payaso had been holding back began to pool in his eyes, and rather than let Phatty see him cry, he turned away to go home.

"Hey, Payaso," Clyde called out. "Why don't you grab that Kindle of yours and come over and show me how to use it?"

Payaso turned to Clyde. "Really? You want me to show you something?" Payaso whispered.

"Yes, really," Clyde responded. "What? Now all of a sudden you don't think you're the smartest cat in town? Despite everything about today, I have to admit …" Clyde cleared his throat and mumbled, "I did have a lot of fun. You're a cool cat. Well, aside from the stroller thing."

Payaso stood frozen, staring over at Phatty, who sat at his door watching Payaso.

"Come on! Hurry up getting your Kindle and come back quick!" Phatty hollered as he turned to head back to his favorite spot.

"Phatty, you want me to come back too?" Payaso asked.

Phatty stopped. "What do you mean, do I want you to come back? Of course I do."

"I just figured, now that you have so many new and cool friends, why would you want me in the way?"

Phatty responded before Clyde could. "Not need you? What do you mean *not need you*? I will always 'need' you, Payaso. You're my first *and* best friend. Nobody could replace you, not even if I made a million new friends. And yes, I said a million." Phatty looked around very proudly. "And maybe some of those million friends will be human ones too."

"A million! Phatty, that is a lot of friends. Do you know how many a million is?" Payaso asked.

"Oh, here we go," Clyde mumbled. "There he is—there's the cat we know! Just skip the math class, go get your Kindle, and get back over here, Payaso. But clean yourself up first. You smell like the boat pond!" He and Stanley giggled, remembering the sight of Payaso falling headfirst into the water.

As Payaso started through his front door, Phatty called to him. "Payaso? Thank you for always believing in me. And for coming with my brothers to find me."

"Phatty …" Payaso started to speak even though his voice was raspy from emotion. "I would go to the moon to find you if I had to. You are my best friend, and I will always believe in you!"

"I love you to the moon, Payaso," Phatty said.

"And I love you there and back," Payaso said matter-of-factly as he disappeared into the darkness of his apartment.

Phatty climbed up on his favorite armchair, happy that everyone was safe and reunited. He looked out on the terrace and then past that out into the park in the moonlight. He realized that Rackie would be looking up at the apartment waiting to see a signal. Jumping down from his chair, Phatty went over to the terrace light switch and flipped it on and off several times in a row, signaling to Rackie across the dark park that Phatty and his friends had all made it home safely.

He looked forward to tomorrow. All was right in the world, according to Phatty.

EPILOGUE

It wasn't long before Payaso sat researching and reciting the best treatment for Birdie. They had all made a pact to work together caring for Birdie until she fully recovered and returned to nature where she belonged. Birdie rested comfortably in her new bed under the couch, and Stanley was out cold in his dog bed. Clyde slept soundly on the windowsill, and Phatty sat perched up on his favorite armchair listening to Payaso recite fact after fact after fact. All was copacetic in Phatty's world, and he couldn't remember the last time he felt this happy.

All of a sudden, he heard a loud crash coming from his mom's bedroom.

"What the heck?" Phatty's mom screamed at the sound of plastic toys, bells, and metal cans crashing to the floor. All of the animals sprang up from their resting positions and looked toward the bedroom door.

"Oops!" Phatty laughed, realizing immediately that they had forgotten the final booby trap! Toy after toy continued to fall down on their mom's head.

"Boooooys!" she hollered as she tripped over the dozens of

little balls and toys now surrounding her feet. "I don't know what I am going to do with all of you," she laughed as she bent down to clean them all up.

The whole family burst out in laughter.

It had been a great day—one full of adventure, surprise friendships, and memories that they would cherish forever. In fact, it was among the best days of Phatty's life.

He climbed up on his favorite armchair, snuggled into its gooshy cushions contentedly, and sighed with happiness. Everyone was safe and reunited.

Phatty looked around at his crew. Clyde sat giving himself a bath, his sleek, tigerlike demeanor and his beautiful green eyes looking delighted. Stanley lay asleep in his bed, white fur settled just so. And Payaso, as usual, was nose-deep in his Kindle, stretched out on the sofa. Phatty knew by now that Wally was safely back at the zoo and that Max would come to visit tomorrow. Everything seemed perfect again in Phatty's world.

As Phatty sat on his favorite chair observing everyone he loved so much, he couldn't help but wonder what this crazy bunch would conquer next.

But after today, he knew that together they could do just about anything.

NOTE FROM THE AUTHOR

There are so many people who supported me along the way in this process that it would take about a thousand trees to have enough paper to properly thank each and every one of you. Thank you to everyone who has read the book and offered to host book parties, sell the book, and recommend the book. Please know that all of you mean so much to me. A special thank-you to the following people who not only made this book possible but made a huge difference in the story:

Michael Shulman
Craig Saavedra
Joaquin Sedillo
Isabel Rivera
Cardinal Timothy Dolan
Felice Schachter
The Hartlelius Family
The Fedeli Family
The Reiter Family
The Curley Family
Kathi Wittkamper
Carmen Unanue
Jane Williams
Lauran Tuck
Eileen O'Mara
Helen Dunning
Jeanette Staluppi
Gary Sunshine
Edgardo Miranda-Rodriguez
Lisa Shamus
Nolan Estes
Arthur Ainsberg
Heather Schroder
Madeleine Metzler
Ira Rosen
Pat Simmons
Gianna Delgado
Bettina Alonso
Raquel Quinones
Annie Jennings, PR
JKS Communications
David Ushery
Michelle Ruiz
The Albanese Family
The Antia Family
The Corley Family
The Entire Unanue Family
Joe Zwilling